THE DAIRY FARMER'S DAUGHTER

SARAH WILLIAMS

 Serenade Publishing

Publisher's Note: This is a work of fiction. Names, characters, places, and incidents are a product of the author's imagination. Locales and public names are sometimes used for atmospheric purposes. Any resemblance to actual people, living or dead, or to businesses, companies, events, institutions, or locales is completely coincidental.

Cover design: Lana Pecherczyk.

ISBN 978-0-6480463-3-2 Print Edition

ISBN 978-0-6480463-2-5 Digital Edition

Serenade Publishing

www.serenadepublishing.com

To my father, Paul.
Once a farmer, always a farmer.
Also to Lynda, for taking care of him for us.

SARAH WILLIAMS

LOVE STORIES THAT WILL ROPE YOU IN

CHAPTER 1

The light shining from the house beckoned Freya Montgomery home with the promise of a refreshing shower and a hot coffee. The sun was just peeking over the mountain range as she slogged through the rain-soaked mud back to the house. Bird calls, combined with the unmistakable bellowing of cows, became an animal symphony.

Even in the dark, she knew the way home from the milking shed. She knew exactly where the path turned and where the paved steps began. She had been travelling this track her entire life, as a baby in her mother's arms and now as a grown woman working the dairy farm and business with her family.

Denver, their ever-faithful dog, climbed the stairs and reached the terrace first. He slurped water from his bowl before plonking himself down by the door. His tail thumped on the floorboards and his jowls almost seemed like they were grinning.

Freya reached down and scratched the Kelpie's head. "Good boy, Denny."

Letting the dog return to stand sentinel at the front door, she yanked off her muddy boots and thick, waterproof jacket. She opened the door and stepped inside the warm house. A fire was blazing in the hearth, and the welcoming smell of brewing coffee filled the air.

"Freya?" Her sister, Greer, was crouched at the fridge, the door wide open. "Did you eat all the blueberries? I wanted to make muffins."

Freya padded softly over in her thick woollen socks and joined her sister on the floor. "I had to hide them from Dad. I saw him eyeing them off last night." Freya reached her arm into the refrigerator, pushed aside a loaf of bread, and pulled out a large plastic container of plump berries.

"Thanks. I really didn't want to make scones again." Greer took the punnet and the women stood up.

Greer hunched her shoulders and pinched the tip of her nose with her fingers. "Sis, you know I love you, but you stink. Please get out of my kitchen."

Freya stepped closer and drew in a long breath. "Don't you like my perfume? Eue de Bovine?"

Greer squirmed and pushed her away.

"Geez, I'd have thought you'd be used to the smell after all these years," Freya said.

"You guys do the milking, I do the cooking. That's the agreement." She wagged her finger, but the smile on her face was the same spirited one she used whenever they played their sister-squabble games.

Freya wrapped her arms around Greer, rubbing the smell onto her sister's clothes. "And we all love your cooking, Sis." She planted a big sloppy kiss on her cheek before letting go.

"Morning, girls." Their mother, Nina, entered the room and came over to kiss both her daughters. Freya inhaled her mother's floral perfume as she hugged her, the smell adding another level of comfort to the embrace.

"How did the milking go this morning?" Nina asked her.

"Good. Dad's waiting for the vet to come and preg-test the heifers." Freya made two cups of coffee as she continued chatting to her mum and Greer worked around her, busily baking.

The cows at Emerald Hills were milked twice a day, every single day, even in winter when the temperature in Maleny dropped close to zero. Even then the cows would still line up in front of the shed, waiting for their meals, milking, and daily check-ups.

"There you go." Greer placed a plate with four pieces of toast spread with a thin layer of Vegemite on the table for the women.

"Thank you, darling." Her mother's voice was full of affection and gratitude. The women sat down and took a piece each.

"Will you have time to help us set out the food for Boyd's wake today?" Nina asked Freya.

"I've got a few things on. Updating the website is doing my head in. I can't figure out the back-end coding. I think I need to call in an expert."

Greer sat next to her and sipped her coffee. "I thought you were the expert. You know all that technical stuff - that's what you're paid for."

"Hey, I'm the marketing department, not IT. I can do social media in my sleep, but HTML codes are practically a different language." She bit into her toast and let the yeasty taste of the vegemite fill her mouth. "What time does the funeral start again?"

Nina glanced at her watch. "The funeral is at one at the church. We'll need to set up the tables and food before it starts."

"Okay." Freya nodded. "I still think it's good of you to do all this for Boyd."

"Well, his son didn't seem very interested. If we'd left it up to him, I doubt there would be a funeral at all." Nina shrugged.

"Who is this son? Is he coming today?" Greer leaned forward. The girls knew so little about their neighbour, even though he had lived next door to them his entire life.

"His name is Justin. He's about Greer's age," Nina said. "I've spoken to him a couple of times about the plans and have invited him. He didn't say for sure whether he would come or not."

"It's his dad. What kind of person doesn't want to go to their own father's funeral?" Greer screwed up her face.

"Do you remember him at all? Has he ever been back?" Freya asked. She had heard the story that Boyd's wife had only lived with him on the farm for a few years. The marriage had fallen apart, and she had taken their young son to Brisbane when he was only four years' old.

"He was a sweet-natured child, but we didn't see them much. I tried to be neighbourly to his mother, Barbara, but I had a toddler of my own and was pregnant, and there was so much going on here, with Bill starting the factory and everything. Dairying is a hard life—you know that. Not everyone is cut out for it."

"But he never came back? Not even for a visit?" Greer asked.

Nina shook her head. "No, Boyd was alone until the day he died. Poor man. He put his farm ahead of everything, even his own health. He literally killed himself by working too hard."

The girls nodded in agreement. Over the years Boyd had grown frailer, but when people had tried to help him, his pride got in the way and he waved their generosity off.

"We have to make sure Dad stays healthy and takes more breaks. He's not getting any younger," Freya said. She and her father both shared the same love of the land and animals. He had tried to send her away to the city, but it hadn't suited her, the hustle and bustle. She had returned to Maleny after university with a business degree and a plan to help the growing family business.

Freya swallowed the last of her toast and stood. "I better get going so I can help you then. You know people will show up early for a yarn."

"They sure will. Thanks for all your help organising this, girls. I really appreciate it," Nina said and kissed each of them in turn.

"No problem, Mum. What's family for?" Greer smiled. "I'll be up soon, but first I'm going to change into something that doesn't smell like I've been cleaning out manure."

Freya laughed. "Good idea. That wouldn't be very nice for the customers."

Out the window, the sun was shining its golden rays over the hills, warming the dew from the grass and promising a glorious day ahead on the Sunshine Coast Hinterland.

CHAPTER 2

*J*ustin would have preferred to stay in the city and pretend it was an ordinary day. A day that didn't include a funeral for a father he'd barely known.

When he'd discussed it with his mother on the phone the night before, she'd been sympathetic. "I'd go, but people might recognise me as his ex-wife and I don't want to make it all about me."

"I don't want to go," he spoke thinly around the avocado-seed-sized lump in his throat. "I haven't seen him in more than twenty years. But I have a feeling that I'll regret it if I don't."

"You don't have to stay long, stand at the back of the church and don't draw attention to yourself."

And that was just what he intended to do. He had purposely arrived at five minutes to one.

He hadn't counted on the parking lot being full and having to leave the car all the way up the road.

He ran his palms down his trousers as he neared the open church doors. He was clean-shaven and smartly dressed in his nicest work suit. If anyone found out who he was, at least he'd look the part of a grieving son.

Not that he was.

He didn't remember anything about Boyd Wheeler. Or living in Maleny. All he knew was that Boyd had never tried to be a part of his life after he'd left the farm. Not a visit, not a phone call, not even an old-fashioned letter in the mail.

Rejection was all he knew from his father. So why did he feel the need to come? To be here for the man who had never been there for him?

Boyd had never attended a soccer game, an awards ceremony, or even his school graduation. His stepfather had though. His stepfather had been his dad, the male role model in his life and, alongside his mother, had raised him to be the man he was today.

The man that knew he was better than Boyd Wheeler. He would never reject his family. He could not miss this funeral and risk spending even a minute regretting it.

He nodded at the usher in the foyer who handed him the program. He looked down at the candid shot of Boyd. It looked like it had originally been a group shot and the designer had cropped everyone else out of it and zoomed in.

Justin had expected him to have aged and changed from the photos his mother had kept, but he wasn't prepared for the frail old man who stared back at him.

He could have been mistaken for a much older man, not the fifty-four-year-old he was when he'd died of a heart attack.

Justin studied the features of the former Wheeler patriarch. Wrinkles, receding hairline, and age spots all over his face. He studied it for a hint of resemblance, but whether it was because he couldn't see it, or simply didn't want to, nothing jumped out.

He followed the sound of chatter into the main church hall and paused abruptly to stare around the crowded room filled with people he didn't recognise.

He shuffled past the crowd and tried to remain discreet in a darkened corner. Then he caught a woman squinting at him and knew he had been spotted. She was his mother's age, dressed in a smart black suit with long greying hair, and was walking directly towards him.

"Justin?" She had a kind, sweet voice.

He nodded and gave her his best leave-me-alone smile.

"I'm Nina Montgomery. We spoke on the phone."

He recognised her voice now. The quiet determination she had used to convince him to have a funeral. Justin had wanted to send the body straight to the crematorium, without a service of any kind.

"Oh, hi." He shook her hand, the polite, well-mannered man his mother had raised taking over. "Thank you for doing all this."

"Of course. Everyone deserves a good send-off." She looked at him with eyes full of sympathy. "Now, come sit with us, and I'll let the minister know he can start."

He followed her to the front pew, conscious of people pointing and whispering around him. So much for not being recognised. His mother had warned him what small towns were like; everyone knew everyone and all their business. Justin liked his privacy and hated being the centre of attention. That's why he worked on computers all day. Alone.

"These are my daughters, Greer and Freya, and my husband, Mark," Nina said, pointing to two attractive young women and an older man, who nodded back. They all had warm smiles and friendly faces.

One of the women shifted over so he could sit beside her. He took the spot with a tight smile and sat on the cushioned bench.

The minister started speaking and it struck Justin that he didn't know if Boyd had been a religious man. His father and Barbara had been married in a church in Brisbane, surrounded by her family and friends. Boyd's own parents had died young and his mother had told him that there had been no one else to invite from his side. His funeral was the opposite, with standing room only and a sombre silent congregation.

All Justin knew of his father was what his mother had told him. His birthday was 12 December; he owned a small dairy farm in Maleny. Barbara had been notified of his death—still named as his next of kin after all these years.

It had taken twenty-six hours before anyone had realised Boyd was missing. He was only found when the farm manager had gone looking for him to help with the afternoon milking.

Boyd Wheeler had died alone.

Justin turned his head to take in the strangers sitting around him. Were all these people Boyd's friends? Had he been able to fill his life with mateship, so he didn't feel the loss of his son and family?

The minister invited Mark Montgomery to deliver the eulogy, and Justin watched as Nina's husband stood behind the lectern and addressed the congregation.

Mark had a deep voice and a serious face. "Boyd and I were neighbours all our lives. He was a couple of grades above me at Maleny school, and I remember him being a quiet but astute student. He dropped out when he was fifteen to dairy with his dad, who then died a couple of years later. His mother was already gone, so he was on his own."

There was nodding and murmurs from the crowd, as though everyone was pausing to remember Boyd's parents and think about their own.

"He married Barbara in Brisbane, and he brought her here to live. They had one child, a son, Justin."

He felt the stares on the back of his neck and sunk lower in his seat.

Mark continued in his solid, stable voice. "They were happy for a few years, but as often happens, dairying wasn't the life for Barbara, so she and Justin moved back to the city to be closer to her family. Boyd stayed on and ran the farm faithfully. He employed many locals over the years including Fred, his farm manager, and even the odd European back-packer. Like the rest of us, Boyd endured the ups and downs of the dairy industry, and when others gave up and left the land, he held onto his farm and cows, because that was the kind of bloke Boyd was."

Justin looked down at the picture again. His father had lived simply and quietly. If he was lonely, it was his own damn fault. If he had wanted to be in his son's life, he could have been. Justin and Barbara would have found a place for him in their lives. Barbara had called and written often over the years.

But Boyd had never answered their calls or letters. He had never come to visit or asked them to visit him.

But he had never even tried.

"Boyd was a steadfast part of the community. His loss is our loss. He will be missed." The church choir started singing as Mark returned to the pew.

He paused briefly to shake Justin's hand. "If you need anything, just ask us. Everyone here knew and liked Boyd."

"Thank you," Justin said. "I appreciate that."

Another sermon was read and then four men, including Mark, hoisted the coffin off the table and walked slowly down the aisle. "Amazing Grace" played through the speakers, and Justin felt emotion rise within him.

A warm hand slipped into his and he turned to see Freya, the blonde daughter, beside him. She squeezed his hand and encouraged him to walk behind the coffin. Stepping out into the sunshine, he was grateful for the clean air after the thick atmosphere in the chapel. He watched as the casket was carefully loaded into the hearse.

"He's going to the crematorium," Freya whispered near his ear. "Do you want to go?"

Justin watched as the door was closed, and he could no longer see the shiny brown casket through the tinted glass window. "No. I said my goodbye years ago."

He turned away from the car, needing to focus on something else, anything other than the car taking his father's body away to be burnt.

He looked at Freya. The light streaming through the trees gave her an ethereal quality. As though seeing her for the first time, he was captivated by her beauty. The scattering of freckles across her nose. The warm brown of her eyes and the soft blonde of her hair.

"I'm sorry for your loss. All of it." She smiled at him, and something passed between them. Empathy perhaps, understanding.

"Thanks." For a long moment, they held each other's gaze, and beneath the buzz of his nerves, he sensed another connection being made. Something stronger than empathy. An alliance of sorts, that together they would get through this.

Then the crowds gathered. By now, the whole congregation had discovered who he was and wanted to learn more about Boyd's son and whatever had happened to him. Freya squeezed his hand before letting go and disappearing into the throng of people.

"Will you be staying long?" Deborah Deslop asked Justin as they sipped tea on the terrace outside the church

For what felt like the hundredth time today, Justin smiled politely and declared he was only up for the funeral.

"What will happen to the farm?" Mr Deslop leaned in. He had introduced himself as the town's bank manager.

"I'm not sure. I have an appointment with Boyd's lawyer this afternoon." He glanced at his watch, noting he still had plenty of time before he would have to leave. He had spotted Webster's Law Firm on Maple Street as he had driven through the one-street town. He had been surprised to see so many people out and about, sitting at the trendy-looking cafes, drinking coffee and reading papers.

Mr Deslop pulled out his card from his jacket pocket and presented it to Justin. "Your father banked with us his entire life. My details are all there if you need anything handled."

"Thank you." Justin put the card in his pocket.

Accounts would have to be closed and things sorted out, just as soon as he talked to Stephen Webster. Justin was hoping he could leave it all in the lawyer's capable hands. He planned on heading back to the city tonight and being back at work tomorrow morning.

"What do you do for a crust?" Mr Deslop asked.

Justin drew in a breath, once more feigning brightness. "I'm a software developer."

"Oh. Do you work for a big company in Brisbane?" Mrs Deslop looked like she was memorising the conversation, no doubt so she could tell all her friends at bridge.

"I freelance. I just finished a project for a travel agency chain." Justin loved talking about his work, but people didn't usually understand the technical aspects involved.

A woman's melodic laughter rang out, and Justin lifted his head in the direction the sound came from. Freya was grinning widely, deep in conversation with some people he hadn't met.

His pulse quickened as he studied her profile.

"I saw that you met Freya Montgomery already," Mrs Deslop said. "She's around your age. She has a sister, and two cousins too."

"Yes, her mother introduced us earlier," he replied and drained his teacup, wishing it was coffee.

"She works on computers too." Mrs Deslop nodded, her eyes wide. "You two would have lots to talk about."

"Really?" He nodded, lips tight.

"She does all the marketing and business development for Emerald Hills," Mr Deslop said. "It's become quite the empire, thanks to her."

Justin raised his eyebrows. She is the one behind Emerald Hills? He had seen their catchy advertisements online. Freya couldn't be more than twenty-five, but he of all people knew that hard work and a keen eye could achieve great things—especially using today's technology and social media. In a world of Insta-fame and YouTube streaming, anyone could become a star, and almost anything could go viral.

Mrs Deslop caught Freya's eye and waved her over. Freya excused herself from the group and walked toward them. Justin watched as she smiled and nodded at various acquaintances along the way.

"Thanks for coming." Freya hugged the older woman and shook her husband's hand. "How are you?"

They exchanged pleasantries, all the while Justin watched her. She was pretty, really pretty.

Mrs Deslop placed a chubby hand on his shirt.

"Justin has just been telling us about his job. He's a software developer."

Freya turned inquisitive eyes on him. "Really? I would be very interested in talking to you, if you don't mind."

"Sure." He gestured to the table laden with refreshments. "I was just going to get another one."

"Nice to see you," she said to the Deslops who smiled and waved them off.

Freya leaned in close to Justin, and he felt her breasts brush his arm. "I'm dying for a coffee."

The sigh escaped his lips before he could stop it. "Me too."

"Let's get all the good stuff before it's gone," Freya said as they arrived at the table full of sweets and savouries. "Have you tried the carrot cake?"

"I haven't had a chance to eat anything yet."

"We can't let you go hungry. Mum and Greer spent hours cooking up this feast, so you have to at least try a taste."

Dutifully, he picked up a plate and loaded it with everything she pointed out, then watched as she poured two cups of coffee. He was just about to tell her to make his black when she lifted the milk jug.

"This milk is direct from Boyd's farm. It makes even instant coffee taste amazing." She poured it into the cups and stirred. "Let's go out the back. It's such a beautiful day, and I need some vitamin D." She carried the cups while he held the plate piled with food and followed her through a side-gate.

The day was warm despite being the middle of winter.

Freya led him to a bench seat under a huge tree. They sat separated only by the plate of food and their mugs of coffee.

"What a great spot," he said as he gazed down onto the town below.

Freya shifted closer to him and extended a long slender arm. "Do you see the supermarket?"

He inhaled her floral scent and looked where she pointed. "That big building?"

"That's it. They sell all sorts of local produce in there. Tourists come to Maleny just to shop there."

Justin noted the pride in her voice.

"Over there is the community centre." She pointed across the street at an impressive two-storey building. "Lots of functions happen in there, including the dance school recitals, movie nights, and all the other events Maleny has on. There's always something going on."

"Have you always lived in Maleny?" He slid her a sideways glance.

"Sure have. I was born in the local hospital." She pointed in another direction where trees were heavily planted. "And I went to the local primary and high school. You can see the primary school, just up there."

He studied where she pointed and could just make out an oval and cluster of buildings. "If Mum hadn't left, that's where I would have gone to school." The words escaped him before he could stop them.

"Yep. You probably would have played soccer for the Maleny Rangers and worked at the supermarket in the holidays."

He frowned at her. "How did you know I played soccer?"

She laughed. "Most boys play either soccer or rugby, and you don't look like a rugby player to me."

Warmth spread through him. "Really? What else do I look like to you?"

She tapped a finger against her glossy lips and furrowed her brow. "You're not a farm boy, so you couldn't fix a tractor. But you are smart. You would have gone to university in Brisbane and climbed the ranks quickly. Judging by that fancy suit, you probably earn a descent salary too."

He looked down at his black jacket and trousers. She was right, of course. How different his life would have been if he had stayed in the country. If, instead of spending his weekends in front of a computer, he had been on the farm learning about cows and machinery. Working with his hands and helping to produce a product that fed the nation.

"What's your story then, Freya Montgomery? Have you ever been to the big smoke?"

She threw him a wide smile, and he got the impression she never let anything bother her. "Actually, I studied business management at the University of Queensland at St Lucia for a year. Then I transferred to the University of The Sunshine Coast and changed to business marketing."

He gave her an apologetic look. She appeared too good to be true. "Are you married?"

"I'm not married, no." She blushed. It was adorable and did nothing to curb his burgeoning attraction.

A young boy came running over then, and threw himself at Freya.

"Nana gave me chocolate cake," he exclaimed and licked his lips. His mouth was smeared with chocolate, and Freya reached into her pocket and pulled out a handkerchief and started wiping it away.

Justin's heart sank. The child's resemblance to Freya was unmistakable and she had a tender, delicate way with him.

The boy looked up at Justin curiously. "Who are you?"

Freya bounced him on her knee. "This is Justin. He's Boyd's son."

"Sorry your dad died," the boy said before sliding off Freya's lap and giving Justin a quick hug. "He was nice."

Justin patted the boy's back, overcome by the affectionate gesture. "Thank you. What's your name?"

"Finn. I'm in grade one," he said, very seriously.

"Really? What's your favourite subject?"

Finn furrowed his brow and paused, deep in thought. "Lunch."

Freya laughed and pulled him over, so she could snuggle into the boy's neck. He giggled and squirmed before breaking free and running back around the house.

"Finn is my cousin's son. His dad owns the local butchery."

Justin couldn't help the relief that swept through him. "So, he's not yours?"

She shook her head and smiled. "No. I'm so single I still live at home with my sister and parents."

His heart did a somersault and his adolescent crush took on a new level.

"You should come for dinner tonight. Mum's already cleared out Boyd's fridge."

"Thanks, but I'm going back to Brisbane after my appointment with the lawyer."

"How are you going to find time to go to the farm as well?"

"I'll organise someone to clean out Boyd's things. I don't plan on keeping the property."

Freya's face fell. "But you only just got here. You have to at least see the farm before you leave. It's where you were born." She turned pleading eyes on him. "Please, stay tonight and come to dinner."

He liked the way she didn't ask a lot of questions. She never referred to Boyd as his father either. It was a simple thing, but he appreciated it.

He gave a sigh of surrender. She made him feel warm and wanted with her interest and he hated to disappoint her. "Fine, okay. One night."

Her whole face lit up with her smile. "You won't regret it. Greer is a chef, and her pasta is amazing."

The delight on her face made his insides tumble, and he wondered if this was such a good idea. His life was in Brisbane. He didn't need any ties to Maleny. Not his father's property and certainly not this farm girl.

Even if she had managed to turn one of the worst days of his life into one of the best.

CHAPTER 3

*J*ustin closed the file of paperwork in front of him and leaned back resolutely in his chair.

"So as you can see," the lawyer, Stephen Webster, said with a sombre expression, "the farm has potential. Boyd never wasted money and he always sought good advice. You are the only beneficiary, so the question now is will you keep it or get rid of it?"

In Justin's mind there was no choice. He didn't want to be a dairy farmer; he wouldn't know where to start. Maleny seemed a nice enough town to visit, maybe spend a long weekend, but he enjoyed the bustle of the city, the fine dining and plentiful entertainment. And his family was there. His mother, stepdad, brother and sister. "How quickly can we get it on the market?"

Boyd's lawyer was a plump man, nearing retirement age. He ran his hand over his bald freckled head. "I've already done some asking around and to be honest there's not much interest in a working dairy farm these days. Not when the price of milk is so low and the major supermarkets are keeping up this price war. Boyd had a good thing going with Emerald Hills. All his milk went to them." Stephen scratched his chin. "There are enough employees to keep it going as it is. I know the manager is a good man—you can trust him. Or there is the option to lease it out."

"Lease it out?" Justin leaned forward. "Do you mean the land?"

"No, the whole thing. Milking shed, stock, everything. A dairy that's already established will often take on leases for other properties. I can ask around, I'm sure we could find someone. The Montgomerys might even be interested."

It wasn't an ideal situation, but worth considering. "I guess I could lease it out until a buyer comes along. Ideally though, I'd rather sell it. Leasing could create other problems along the way, not to mention the tax implications."

"Yes, the government always wants their bit. I'll look into the leasing and come back to you."

Justin rose and shook Stephen's hand. "I appreciate that, and you have all my contact details now."

"Of course, and again, my sincerest condolences."

"Before I go ..." Justin paused. "Do you have a key to get into the house? I've decided to stay the night."

The older man raised his eyebrows before reaching into his desk drawer. He handed Justin a simple silver key. "Nina Montgomery has been keeping an eye on the place. The power is still on and it runs on tank water. You should be comfortable there."

"Thank you." Justin left the office and walked out onto the main street. It was after five now and the road had quietened down. The sun was lowering and bringing with it a chilly night breeze. Nevertheless, he decided to walk and clear his head before going to the farm.

He wandered down the wide footpath, noting the huge deciduous trees and quaint storefronts. As well as art galleries, cafés, and fashion stores, there was a children's playground, a bakery and even a barbershop with old-fashioned red and white striped poles out the front.

He passed the butcher's shop, the old-time building with historic, rustic appeal, and wondered if that was where Finn's father worked.

He paused to study the display at a bookstore

café. Country scenes adorned the book covers. He shoved his hands in his pockets. He could rarely walk past a bookstore without buying something, his love for literature so strong. His mother liked to boast that he had been able to read before he started school. Had his mother brought him here? Had they bought books from this shop?

It was closed now, so he decided to come by in the morning and order a coffee, then he could have a good look around while he waited.

He crossed the street and wandered back towards his car. The evening air revived him and the walking stretched out his tight muscles. Maleny had all the essential stores, and the larger cities of Maroochydore and Caloundra, where shopping centres and department stores flourished, were within an hour's drive down the winding range.

Deciding he better grab a toothbrush and tooth-paste, since he had brought nothing with him for his impromptu overnight stay, he headed into the supermarket and picked up a basket.

The deli section Freya had mentioned did not disappoint. Sliced meats and antipasto were on full display, and his mouth watered at the array. The bakery section was just as enticing with all sorts of cakes and slices. Bread of varying shapes and sizes lined display shelves with a selection of fillings including fruit, nuts and seeds.

The colourful array of fruit and vegetables, especially the organic section, which was just as big, made him want to focus on eating better, healthier food. Living in the city, he often skipped meals or ate out, unless he was at his mum's house. She always insisted on cooking a homemade meal.

He put a banana and an apple in his basket, then found a toothbrush and toothpaste and headed towards the checkout. As he waited in line, he spied the display of coffee beans with the unfamiliar Maleny coffee logo on brown paper packaging. He collected a large bag and added it to his purchases. He knew it wouldn't be much but still felt good for contributing to the local economy. Maleny didn't seem that bad after all; no wonder it drew thousands of tourists every year.

The GPS system on his phone directed him out of town, and he was surprised how quickly the suburban sprawl turned to lush, green pastures and quiet country roads.

The white milk-can indicated the driveway he was to turn down. He slowed to take in every detail of Boyd's property. The winding dirt track skirted wood and wire fences. At one point, he drove over a flowing creek which jogged something in his memory, though he couldn't think what.

As the car climbed a small hill, he took one hand off the wheel and brushed it down his thigh. It was stupid to be nervous, but despite being the new owner of the property, he was. Would he feel Boyd's presence in the house? Would he learn something about the man who had always been a stranger?

The setting sun still threw enough light for Justin to see the old iron milking shed when he came to the top of the rise. A mixture of black and white cows and some caramel-browns grazed contentedly in the grassy pasture. To his untrained eye, Justin could only presume they were in as good a condition as Stephen had suggested.

He continued down the road, eager to reach the house before dark. The car's headlights illuminated a small house, and he parked in the carport, next to a dirty work ute.

It was quiet, apart from the soft mooing of cattle. The path to the house was short and when he reached the wooden front door, he used his key to enter.

He switched on a light and looked around the cosy living room. The couch was aged but promised comfort. Beyond it was a basic kitchen and dining room. A quick look in the fridge confirmed it had been emptied.

He ventured farther into the house and found a basic if somewhat dated bathroom. There were two small bedrooms, each filled with a single bed and dresser. The main bedroom was at the end of the hall. He turned on the light and looked around. The floral bedspread and lace doylies reminded him of his grandmother's house.

The room had a distinctly feminine feel to it. He sat on the queen-sized bed and breathed in the lingering scents.

This was where Boyd had slept, where he had lived.

A silver-framed photograph on the bedside table caught Justin's attention, and he picked it up for a closer look. He recognised his mother dressed in a pale dress, holding a newborn baby in her arms. A younger version of Boyd stood next to her. He looked handsome in his suit, not yet wrinkled and weary.

His mother had said they were happy for a time. This must have been taken at the peak of that happiness. Perhaps his own christening, given the state of their dress. The young couple were still in love and proud to be new parents of a healthy child. They had no idea it would all fall apart in just a matter of years.

After freshening up in the bathroom, Justin locked the house and followed the directions Freya had given him to her house.

The tree-lined driveway ended, and he was presented with a double-storey, white weatherboard Queenslander-style house. Soft light filtered through the open windows and chattering voices made their way out to him.

"He has his father's ears, don't you think?" He heard Nina say.

"I never paid much attention to Boyd's ears, but I agree there is a similarity," Mark replied.

"I was surprised so many people came." Another voice—not Freya, but similar. "He wasn't even a member of the church."

A red dog suddenly ran up to Justin and he jumped back. It sat on its haunches and looked up expectantly, then when Justin didn't pat him straight away, the dog raised his paw.

Justin bent down to pat the dog but the moment he touched its head the dog flopped onto its back and spread his legs in expectation of a belly rub.

Freya came out to greet him. He was struck by her inviting girl-next-door look in a pair of skinny jeans and a navy sweater. Thick brown Ugg boots completed the comfortable outfit. "He likes you," she said.

"Seems all the Montgomerys are friendly-even the animals." He tickled the dog's belly in an effort not to gawk at the woman in front of him.

Her laughter wrapped around his heart with a soft, gentle warmth. "This is Denver. He's the best farm dog in Maleny." She whistled and the dog jumped into a sitting position, head and ears alert, waiting for her next signal.

She turned back to Justin. "I'm so glad you came." She pressed a kiss to his cheek then put her arm through his and walked him up the stairs, through the terrace and into the house.

Upon entering the living room, he paused while his eyes adjusted to the inside lighting. The room was large with a stone fireplace taking up a great deal of the side wall. Flames roared up the chimney adding an extra layer of warmth to the family home.

Nina wrapped him in a warm embrace. "I'm so glad you came," she echoed Freya's words kindly. "You're in for a treat; Greer's cooking spaghetti putanesca."

He hugged her back. "Thanks for having me. I wish I'd thought to bring something."

"That's okay. We have everything we need."

"Hi Justin." Greer waved from the kitchen where

she was busy at the counter, and he saw pots bubbling on the stove.

He greeted her and was struck by the similarity between the two sisters. He hadn't really been paying attention before, at the church.

Mark took his turn next and shook Justin's hand, his warmth immediate and genuine. "Good to see you again. Were you happy with the service?"

"Yes, it was fine. Thank you all for everything. I was surprised to see so many people turn up."

"This community always pulls together when something like this happens. I'm only sorry I didn't have more to say about Boyd. I wish I had known him better."

Justin nodded. *Don't we all?*

Mark sank into a La-Z-Boy and waved Justin onto the couch next to him. Freya sat quietly nearby.

"Justin, can I get you a drink? Dinner isn't far-off," Nina said.

Justin glanced at the coffee table where a can of beer sat on a paper coaster. "A beer would be great, thanks."

She smiled and nodded at her daughter. "Freya, do you want something?"

"I'll have a beer too, thanks Mum."

Justin glanced at Freya as she curled a denim-clad leg under her body. She looked comfortable and at ease; he wanted to drape an arm around her and feel her soft body against him.

"So, what did you think of the farm? You did go there, right?" she asked.

"I did. Seems comfortable enough."

"Do you remember it? From before you left?"

"Freya, he was only a toddler. No one remembers things when they were that young." Mark smiled fondly at his daughter.

She ignored her father and raised her eyebrows at Justin.

He shook his head. "I'm afraid not."

Nina returned with drinks, and Justin gratefully accepted his beer.

"Justin's staying at the farm tonight." Freya told her mother, who perched on the arm of her husband's chair.

"Oh good. You should stay for a few days and get to know the area."

"No, I should get back to work. But I will need to talk to the staff first. The lawyer said they should be able to keep everything running until we find a buyer."

Mark leaned forward in his chair. "If you're interested in leasing the farm, we'd be keen. I wish we could buy it, but it's not a good time for us right now. Maybe next year though."

Justin sipped his drink thoughtfully. Stephen had said leasing would be easier to do than finding a buyer in this market, but he wanted to keep his options open for a while.

He smiled at Mark. "I need to do some research and find out what it's worth. Is it true that the milk comes here?"

"That's right. Emerald Hills consists of our farm and dairy shed, plus my brother's factory where they pasteurise the milk and make cream, cheese, and yogurt."

"Plus, we've got the cafe, animal farm, and dairy tours," Freya said, and Justin detected more than a little pride in her voice.

"That's quite the enterprise you have," Justin said.

"Emerald Hills has been in the Montgomery family for generations," Nina said. "Our ancestors were some of the original founders of the area. Mark's brother, Bill, wanted to expand the dairy farm, so he started making cheese and commercial-grade milk. Then when Greer was finished cooking school and travelling, she and Freya opened the cafe."

"Greer does all the work—I just come up with the ideas," Freya said.

"So, farm tours and animals too?" He loved how her face brightened up with satisfaction.

"That's for the tourists; they love seeing a working dairy farm in action. We offer them rides on a trailer pulled behind a tractor. They can look inside the factory too and see how Emerald Hills products are made."

Justin gazed in astonishment at Freya-who could just be the perfect woman. Intelligent, creative and entrepreneurial all in one beautiful package.

"We're also a popular wedding venue," she added.

Weddings equalled money. *Well played, Freya.*

"Freya runs the businesses and organises all the events and marketing," Nina explained.

Freya shrugged. "It's a family company. When one part does well, we all succeed."

"You must be very busy," he said.

She shrugged. "I enjoy what I do, and I get to stay on the farm and help my family."

"She still helps with the milking too. Even the morning shifts." Mark beamed.

"I've gotta keep my eye on you," she teased.

Mark leaned forward and placed his elbows on his knees. "It's a difficult life, working on the land. It's not for everyone and it's hard on families. Divorce rates are high, and every year we see more and more kids head off to the big smoke in search of an easier life. One where you get paid a decent wage for your time and effort. A man can end up trapped, owing too much, and then forced to sell, walking away with nothing more than the clothes on his back to show for a lifetime of working all-day, every-day."

Justin's lips thinned. The truth of Mark's words were written on his face. Years of early mornings, hard work, and outdoor life had left him weather-beaten, with a face full of freckles and broken capillaries. Except Mark's family was still intact, his daughters back on the land after taking time away. If Boyd had been forced to choose between his farm and his family, he had chosen wrong.

"Dinner's ready," Greer said as she placed a huge bowl of steaming pasta in the centre of the table.

They all stood and moved to sit around the huge wooden table where a freshly tossed salad was waiting.

"Sit here." Nina motioned to the vacant seat between herself and Freya.

"Everything in the salad is organic and home-grown," Mark explained as he served himself a healthy portion. "We're very health-conscious in this family. Even if we don't always want to be."

"Don't worry, Dad, I made your favourite dessert." Greer winked at him.

Mark looked at her hopefully. "Sticky date pudding?"

Greer nodded.

Freya placed her hand over Justin's and, despite having a mouthful of food, moaned in delight. "Greer's sticky-date pudding is the talk of the town," she explained when she had finally swallowed.

Justin grinned back. "I can't wait. This all looks and smells amazing."

It surprised Justin how at home he felt with the Montgomerys. There were no expectations on him, nor did they try to press him to make a decision about the farm. They chatted easily about his life in Brisbane and their lives in Maleny. When Boyd's name was brought up, they didn't try to make him out as any type of a martyr. He was who he was, and they had accepted Boyd just as they were accepting Justin.

Justin couldn't help looking at Freya. There was not a trace of make-up on her face. Her skin appeared smooth, soft, and radiant. His fingers itched to touch her.

Over dessert, Nina regaled them with stories from the farm—the adventures Freya, Greer, and their various friends and relatives had experienced in their childhood. They'd spent long summer days roaming over the green countryside playing imaginary games, camping by the dam, water-skiing behind the boat, and learning to stand-up paddleboard.

Justin grinned at the picture Nina painted. He could easily imagine a young, sun-bronzed Freya with wild blonde hair blowing in the wind as she ran after a young calf, or leaped, bareback onto her favourite pony.

The Montgomery girls had been raised to climb trees and explore nature, and now had a deep respect and appreciation for all the world had to offer.

When dessert and coffee was finished, Justin sighed contentedly. "Thank you for dinner. That sticky-date pudding really was delicious."

Greer smiled appreciatively as she cleared his plates. "Any excuse to make it. It's my favourite too."

Freya helped her sister to clear the table, and Justin stood to help but she stilled his movement with a warm hand on his arm. "No, you're the guest. Just relax."

"Will you meet with Fred tomorrow?" Mark asked him.

"Fred?"

"The farm manager. He was Boyd's right-hand man. He's been running the place since ..."

Justin nodded. "Yes. I'll find him in the morning and have a chat."

"Fred's a good worker. You can rely on him, and we're here if you need anything," Nina said, her voice reassuring.

"Thank you. I appreciate your kindness," Justin said. "I better get going." He stood and said his goodbyes.

"I'll walk you out." Freya led him to the front door and down to his car.

The cool winter air bit at his cheeks and he gazed up at the cloudless sky, only to be startled by the million sparkling stars of the Milky Way.

"Wow."

"Incredible, aren't they?" she murmured, and he could feel her warmth against his arm. "So clear and so close."

He looked back at Freya, her face shining in the glow of the house lights.

"Thanks for coming," she said softly.

"Thanks for inviting me," he breathed. "Your mum is one of a kind."

Her eyes glittered, and a sly smile tilted the corner of her mouth. "She sure is."

He sank his hands into his pockets. "You're a lot like her."

Freya bumped against him. "I'm hoping that's a compliment."

"Oh, it sure is." He inhaled her fresh, floral scent.

He had always been a sucker for kindness. And pretty girls.

He had never met anyone like Freya before. He liked her slower pace and deep love for her family. The way she was so content in her environment and accepting of other people, even strangers.

"You should give us a chance," she said sweetly.

He raised his eyebrows.

"Maleny. The farm. You might be surprised what you find here."

"I already have been surprised."

She sucked in her lower lip. He breathed out deeply, creating a puff of smoke. "I should go."

Freya reached up on tiptoes and pressed a gentle kiss to his cheek. "Sweet dreams."

He watched as she skipped back up the wooden staircase. Climbing into the car, he already knew that she would be the star of his dreams tonight and they would be sweet. Oh-so sweet.

CHAPTER 4

*J*ustin yawned as he poured boiling water into the coffee plunger he had found in the kitchen cabinet. Maybe he and Boyd did share something in common after all. Even if it was just their taste for freshly brewed coffee.

He had slept surprisingly well last night in Boyd's bed and had woken this morning thinking of Freya. With each sip of coffee, his resolve strengthened. She was a dream. Possible in another life, but not this one. He lived in the city; she lived in the country. Long-distance relationships were hard and he knew it wouldn't work, despite their obvious chemistry. But he would have liked more of that hot, thrilling feeling he experienced whenever their gazes connected.

The responsible thing to do was to leave before things got more complicated. Before he could hit the road though, he needed to see Fred.

He drained the cup of coffee and opened the door to the chilly winter air. Two pairs of over-sized boots—one long rubber, one short leather with laces—stood sentry next to the doormat. He pulled the rubber pair on, grateful he had inherited the same-sized feet. A thick raincoat hung above the boots on a hanger and, as he slipped it on, he hoped it would be thick enough for the crisp weather.

The ground was muddy from an overnight shower, and Justin squelched his way to the milking shed. He followed the line of waiting cows into the shed and stopped to survey the scene. The animals were standing either side of a concrete pit where he saw two men working.

Justin pressed his hand to his nose, the combined stench of animal fluids and manure making him gag. He swallowed hard.

"You must be Justin." A thin man in overalls and a woollen hat approached him.

He nodded. "Are you Fred?"

"Sure am." The men shook hands. "Sorry about your dad. He was a good man."

Justin smiled politely and gestured to the cows,

slotted into stalls divided by metal rails. "So this is how cows get milked."

Fred put his hands on his hips. "Sure is."

Justin listened as Fred explained how the herringbone shed worked. "The cows come in and angle-park themselves side by side, facing away from the centre pit where the milkers work. It's the same on the other side of the pit, so the cows together form a herringbone pattern. A rail at breast-height prevents the cows from moving forward, and they are released together through a gate once milking has finished.

"Each cow has its own individual identification tag. The machines check them while they're milking and track their weight, milk quantity, and anything else we need to track."

A new group of cows entered the stalls and Justin watched as the pumps were cleaned and attached. The technology involved was impressive, and his mind automatically started imagining how it all worked and possible improvements. Perhaps an app?

"What happens if a cow is missing?"

"The machine alerts us. We have built a herd history for ongoing herd management and decision-making. Boyd was always thinking about the farms' long-term future." Something flickered over Fred's face. Grief?

Justin looked around. The milkers were busy doing various jobs and he realised he was taking up Fred's time with all his questions. "I see you're busy," he said. "How can I help?"

Sweat trickled down Freya's neck despite the winter-cool temperature. She slowed her horse, Nutmeg, to a walk and scanned the lush scenery around her. Another beautiful day had dawned on the range, and she was full of hope and joy. Thoughts of Justin filled her every waking minute, and she had found herself up at dawn despite not being on the milking roster.

There was something different about Justin Wheeler. His slim exterior and brawn, his solid shoulders, his thick arms. And those hands. Not callused and rough like those of the country boys she was used to, but still not perfectly smooth either. Nor was he soft around the middle like so many urbanites were. He obviously looked after himself—probably had a gym membership and used it. She certainly enjoyed looking at him and touching him.

She liked the way he reacted to her touch. The spurs of electricity that sparked between them.

She pulled Nutmeg up at the boundary gate and

stretched to unlock it before manoeuvring the horse through and closing it again behind her. Boyd's property, although not as big as Emerald Hills, had a lovely little creek on it that she enjoyed riding along. Boyd had always let her come and go as she liked as long as she followed country ethics and kept gates shut and didn't scare the cows.

She patted Nutmeg's silky brown neck. Nutmeg had seen her through her angsty teenage years, her crushes and first loves. Her passion for animals had never wavered. That's why living in the city had been so hard. No animals to stroke and confide in.

As she approached the house, she spotted two men sitting on the deck—the butterflies of blossoming attraction returned. She waved at Fred, who she had known all her whole life, but it was his companion she was really interested in seeing again.

Justin was dressed like a farmer in thick woollen socks, baggy denims and a fleecy sweater. He stood and walked over to her.

"Morning," she called brightly.

He put his hands on his hips, and she drank him in, all long and lean and man. "Did you ride all this way?"

She nodded. "It's not that far really and Nutmeg needed the exercise." She dismounted gracefully and held the reins.

He looked warily at the animal.

"You can pat her. She won't bite."

He extended a careful hand and gently rubbed the horse's forelock. Nutmeg snorted in appreciation.

"Nice outfit." Freya gestured at his clothes.

"I was helping out in the milking shed this morning."

She smiled widely. "Say no more. Been there, done that." She caught his gaze for a heart-stopping second before he looked away and motioned to the house.

"Can I offer you a coffee? I have fresh milk this morning."

If she wasn't mistaken, his chest might have puffed out just a little. "If it's fresh then I can't turn it down." She tired Nutmeg to a fence post then they walked over to Fred.

She gave the old manager a brief hug. "I didn't get a chance to talk to you yesterday. I saw you at the service and wanted to come and say hi."

Fred looked away, his cheeks pink. "I couldn't stay long. Lots to do here." Emotion thickened his voice.

Justin shuffled behind her, and she moved slightly to include him in the conversation. "Fred's been here for what, twenty-something years?" She patted Fred's hand.

"That's right. In fact, I even remember you." Fred nodded at Justin. "I started working here when you had just learned to walk."

"I bet you have some stories to tell about this one," Freya said and gently bumped against Justin.

Fred gave a throaty laugh.

"I'll get you that coffee." Justin smiled at her.

"I'll help you."

He opened the door for Freya to walk past him.

As they waited for the kettle to boil, Freya leaned on the kitchen table and spoke in a quiet voice, "You know, it was Fred who found Boyd."

Justin paused, hand halfway to the cupboard. "I hadn't even realised. Is he okay?"

Freya shrugged. "Seems to be. He's always been a pretty resilient fellow."

Justin seemed to consider his next words carefully. "If Fred and Boyd were such good friends, why didn't Fred do the eulogy?"

Freya glanced over her shoulder to make sure the manager didn't hear them gossiping about him. "Fred is very reserved; he likes to keep to himself. I saw him at the back of the church during the service, and then he left as soon as it was over."

Justin nodded in reply but didn't ask anything else about him. When the coffee was ready, they went back outside and chatted easily. Fred explained the day-to-day goings on at the farm as well as stock numbers, employees' roles, and what maintenance was required.

Freya offered Justin her family's help, should he need it.

"So, I'm not sure what you plan on doing," Fred said turning to Justin, "but I'm happy to stay on as long as you need me. I've worked here for so long I can't imagine being anywhere else."

Freya watched a softness come over Justin's eyes.

"I do understand that and want to do what's best for everyone. For me, it would be better to sell. You understand my life is in Brisbane. Running a dairy farm is not something I know anything about."

"You could always lease it out," Fred said hopefully.

Justin nodded and stared into his cup as though it held all the answers. "I know, and that is something I'm considering. Mark Montgomery has already shown interest. I'm still thinking about it."

Freya's mood brightened; at least he hadn't made any serious decisions.

Fred stood and stretched his arms over his head. "Well, that's smoko over. Better get back to work."

He shook Justin's hand and gave Freya a wave. "See you later."

Freya and Justin watched him walk away towards the milking shed stop.

"So, what are your plans for today?" Freya turned her attention back to Justin.

"I'm waiting for the washing machine to finish so I can get changed and head to Brisbane." He looked down at his work clothes. "I can't go back like this."

Freya reached across and smoothed the fabric across his chest feeling just briefly his heart pound under her touch. "I don't know. This could be a good look on you."

His face broke into a smile, opening up and bewitching her with its warmth.

A kookaburra screeched overhead, and together they looked towards the old gum trees, their branches bare of leaves. Behind her, Nutmeg whickered as if hurrying her mistress on.

"It's a shame you can't stay any longer." The corner of her mouth twitched. She tucked a stray hair behind her ear. "Don't you want to go through your dad's things before you leave?"

Justin looked at the old house. "I don't think there's anything here I'll want."

"How do you know that if you haven't looked?" She let the words hang in the air as she stood and walked towards her horse. Then, with the ease of a woman who had been riding her entire life, she hoisted herself up into the saddle and took the reins.

Justin walked over and looked up at her. His squint brought small wrinkles around his eyes. They made her heart thump in her chest.

"I can't imagine why you'd want to hurry back to Brisbane when there is so much here you haven't seen. This is your birthright after all." She smiled brightly at him before turning and trotting Nutmeg away.

She wanted him to stay, not just so he could find out who his father had been, but because she wanted the opportunity to get to know him better. Who knew? Maybe he was the breath of fresh air she had been waiting for.

Justin stared at her departing silhouette. His gut churned, and his heart thumped against his ribs—the pull of longing trying to fool him into staying. He had to get out of this town before he got too attached to it, or her.

Freya Montgomery made him feel things, want things he had never dared to want or feel before. Freya Montgomery struck him as the serious, forever type and he wasn't looking for anything serious.

It hadn't worked out for his parents, after all. His mother had always loved living in the city, surrounded by friends and family. Barbara had moved to Maleny for love, but it hadn't been enough. She had always pined for the life and community she had always known.

Of course, that had been a different time. Before Facebook and texting. Hell, before email. Now Justin could keep in touch with his nearest and dearest with a swipe of his finger. He also knew he could work from anywhere. His business was completely mobile and any face-to-face meetings could be done through online conferencing apps. He knew; he had created one himself.

When he had told his half-brother and half-sister that he was inheriting Boyd's property, they had been excited for him, especially Felicity. Ever the romantic, she adored the idea of him owning a sprawling cattle property in the Hinterland. She was still in high school and contemplating university courses.

"The University of The Sunshine Coast has a great reputation, and they offer loads of awesome courses." Had been one of the first things out of her mouth.

His brother, Nick, was in tourism and had a lot

of good things to say about the Sunshine Coast. *"Noosa is practically up the road. Everyone loves Hastings Street for shopping and people-watching, not to mention the beaches up there. They rival the Gold Coast's."*

Mum had been indifferent. *"I'm sure things have changed. I know the Sunshine Coast is growing rapidly,"* she had said, her voice full of emotion and memory. *"Boyd loved living up there and it suited him well."*

It may have suited his father, but a dairy farm? If working in the shed this morning had taught him anything, it was that dairying was hard, messy work and that he should leave it to the professionals. The people who knew what they were doing and enjoyed doing it.

But he couldn't deny the pull he felt to the area. It had planted the seed of possibility which only grew each time he was met with the kindness of a local like Fred or Freya. Not to mention her family. Better people than Nina and Mark Montgomery he was sure he would never meet. No wonder their daughters had turned out so well.

He took a deep breath of fresh country air, and a powerful waft of manure hit his nostrils. He fanned the smell away with his hand and turned towards the house.

Stopping in the kitchen, he cleaned the coffee cups and put them away, then made his way through the house. Maybe he should take the time to go through his father's things. Maybe he would find out why Boyd had never bothered to keep in touch. He must have been curious as to how his only child had turned out.

Money had been deposited into Barbara's bank account every week until Justin turned eighteen. When Barbara had married her second husband, Geoff, three years after returning to the city, she had diverted the funds to an account set up for Justin. It had been Geoff's idea. He was an architect and earned a good salary. He wanted to support all his family, even his stepson. The money had been put to good use, going towards his university costs.

Even though Boyd hadn't known it, he had helped Justin become the man he was today.

As Justin transferred his washing into the dryer and turned the dial, he felt his phone buzzing. It was Stephen Webster wanting to know if Justin was still in town.

"I am actually. I have to hang out here for another"—he glanced at the dryer—"ninety-two minutes."

"Good, because Mark Montgomery called and has officially expressed interest in leasing the farm. I've just emailed you the financials. I really think it's a good deal, at least until we can find a buyer."

Justin scratched his chin. The Montgomerys

were good people; they knew what they were doing. Hell, they had built themselves an empire. He agreed to look the information over and get back to the lawyer.

Maybe he didn't have to cut ties with the town straight away. At least if he leased the farm out, he would have a reason to visit again and check in with the Montgomerys. He would also get to see Freya.

He wouldn't mind doing that.

Four hours, three cups of coffee, and a headache later, Justin had finished looking over the calculations. He had always prided himself on being good with numbers and maths but given the circumstances, he wanted a second opinion, so had emailed everything off to his accountant in the city to look over.

He glanced at his watch; it was after midday, and he was starving. He pulled out his phone to see if there were any cafes closer than those on the main street. Of course, there was, Emerald Hills. His neighbours'—Freya's family's café. Since Greer was the chef, he knew it would be a guaranteed good feed. He collected his wallet and keys and headed to the car.

The drive over was pretty in the daylight, with towering macadamia nut trees lining the road and the verdant green grass under them. Marking the entrance was a big sign which welcomed him to Emerald Hills Farm, Factory, and Café.

He parked, made his way to the entrance, and opened the door to find a very busy dining room with families and couples enjoying delicious-smelling food and the lively atmosphere.

The waitress approached him and asked if he had a booking. When he said no, she frowned and looked down at the thick book full of pencil marks and highlights. Just as he was about to turn and leave, since there weren't any empty tables that he could see, he heard Nina's familiar voice call out to him across the room. She greeted him with a friendly hug and enthusiasm to rival her daughter.

"Are you here for lunch?" she asked. "Freya didn't say anything."

"I was supposed to be driving home by now, but I've been held up, so thought I'd come for a bite to eat." He motioned across the room. "I didn't realise bookings were required."

"You've caught us on a busy day," she said with a smile. "Come with me and I'll make sure you have a meal." She walked him past the counter, which displayed a fine selection of soft and hard cheeses with a sign saying they'd been proudly made on the premises with Emerald Hills milk.

She walked him through a 'no entry' door and

down a corridor with offices and meeting rooms leading off it. She opened another door and they stepped out onto a veranda where a large table for six was unoccupied.

"This is the staff area, but I'll make an exception for you." She pulled out a chair for him. "Now tell me what you'd like to eat. Greer can make just about anything."

He sat on the cushioned, wooden chair and smiled. "What do you recommend?"

"Well, there's all the usual fare like sandwiches and salads, burgers and pasta. But today's special is Greer's famous seafood chowder. She serves it in a cob loaf, and it's something amazing."

Justin felt his mouth water. He was always a sucker for anything seafood, and a chowder would be perfect on a cool day like this. "That sounds delicious. Thank you."

"And something to drink? Perhaps a wine? I have a nice white that goes beautifully with seafood."

Justin took a moment to consider his plans for the rest of the day. It was Friday, after all. No hurry to head back to the city. Especially when he knew traffic would be a nightmare. He nodded. "Why not? Sounds good."

Nina smiled broadly. "Excellent. Let me put your

order through. Is everything else okay? Do you need anything?"

He shook his head, and she left him to enjoy the view. In front of him, cattle grazed in on the gently rolling green hills.

He leaned back into the comfortable outdoor chair and let the cool air envelop him. He already felt better. Lighter. As long as the accountant okayed the deal, the Montgomerys would take over the lease of Boyd's farm and he could get back to the city. Everyone would be happy and able to get on with their lives.

"Couldn't stay away, could you?"

He looked up to see Freya's beautiful face looking back at him.

He smiled. She made him want to smile. A lot. "No. I'm still here. And, since your mum is bringing me out a glass of wine, I don't expect to be driving back to Brisbane tonight."

Freya pulled out the chair next to him and sat down. "Staying another night then? Sounds like we're growing on you after all."

"Seems like it. Every time I try to leave, I find a reason to stay."

She looked at him in such a way that he wanted to bare his soul. To tell her everything about himself and to learn everything about her. And she made him hot. Hot, hard, and messy-brained. Also, a little bit hopeful that he might have a future here after all.

"Do you mind if I eat with you? I'm on my break."

"I'd like that. But you better order your own chowder. I heard it's amazing."

She laughed, and he enjoyed the sound more than he wanted to admit.

After a delicious lunch of chowder and wine, Freya was feeling a little tipsy. The alcohol, the company, and the scenery made for an appealing combination. She and Justin had chatted for hours, discussing everything from their childhood experiences, to hobbies and work. Both being tech heads, they had discussed which software they preferred and what apps would be trending in the future. It had been such a lovely couple of hours—she found herself disappointed it had to end, and even more disappointed that he still planned to leave. He seemed hesitant, however, so she thought up ways to keep him around a little bit longer.

"Why don't you let me show you around Emerald Hills? I'll give you the grand tour?"

He caught her gaze, and for a heart-stopping

second Freya thought he could read her mind. "I'd love that," he agreed.

She led him to the animal farm where they patted the sheep, calves, chickens, and pigs, all the while laughing and giggling like children.

"That's the milking shed"—she pointed out—"but I think you've already seen inside one of those."

He stood beside her. Close. "Can't say I'm in a huge hurry to see another one anytime soon."

"Let's go to the factory then." She took a step ahead, and then paused and placed her hand on his arm. "You do eat cheese, right?"

"That all depends on the cheese and on the company."

Freya giggled and walked her fingers up his muscled arm. "That sounds like a challenge."

She let her hand slide down his arm and curl around his fingers. His eyes deepened, but he didn't remove his hand.

Inside the factory, they walked around the viewing platform where they were separated from the machinery by glass panelling. She explained the manufacturing process of the cheese and yogurt as best as she could remember, having only guided the tour groups a handful of times. But she was surprised how interested Justin seemed to be in everything she said and showed him.

"I had no idea there was so much involved."

Freya pointed to a wall of photos and newspaper articles. which were framed and on display on the back wall.

"My Uncle Bill started the factory. It was his dream." She gazed proudly at the picture of her father, Bill, and their parents when they were much younger.

Justin leaned in closer. "I can see the resemblance."

"You stay here and read all about dairying in Maleny while I go get the cheese."

He nodded, still intently reading the articles.

In the adjoining staff kitchen, she put together a small tasting platter. As she was carrying it out, her uncle called her name from the office next door.

"Isn't that Justin Wheeler?"

"Yes, it is. We've just been touring the factory, and now we are going to try some of this fine food." She looked fondly at his lined weather-beaten face.

"Make sure he tries the camembert. It's a particularly good batch. And I think you should take this." He opened the fridge door and pulled out a bottle of wine. "It will bring out the flavours of the cheese."

She took the bottle before pressing a quick kiss to his cheek. "Thanks, Uncle Bill."

She returned to the room and found Justin still reading about the old butter factory.

He turned when he heard her approaching. "Maleny's history is so interesting. I had no idea."

"I know. As a child I had no interest at all, but it's part of what makes this town so great." She put the platter and wine on the table and poured them each a glass. She handed him one. "Since you're not driving anywhere tonight."

They clinked their glasses together and took a swallow before sitting at the table to enjoy the cheese. She pointed out what was what, then cut him off a piece and handed it to him.

He groaned. "This is so good. Between this and your sister's cooking, how on earth do you stay so slim?"

She laughed. "Trust me, it's not easy."

"Well, whatever you're doing, keep doing it." His voice was honey smooth; she hadn't noticed the velvet tones yesterday. Heat rose up her neck, and a tingle coursed through her body.

She cut him another sample and their fingers brushed as she handed it to him.

She sucked in a breath as her gaze fell to his mouth. She wanted so badly to kiss him, to feel his lips on her mouth. On her body.

He leaned forward, and she could smell the fruity wine on his breath. He was so close. "Freya."

The door to the room burst open as a group of Japanese tourists entered, chatting noisily.

The moment broken, Freya leaned back and laughed. Justin squirmed slightly in his chair before joining her, laughing.

CHAPTER 5

*T*he afternoon sun warmed her as they left the factory. Freya let her hand brush Justin's briefly and when he didn't object, she slipped her fingers between his. The grin he sent her made her heart thump so loud she was surprised he couldn't hear it.

She led him down the path marked 'private'. She wanted to share things with him, experience things with him, do things with him.

"Where are you taking me?" He had a lightness in his voice.

She squeezed his hand, enjoying the feel of his touch. "You'll see."

He signed. "There is something about this place. It's almost magical."

Freya breathed in deeply, the scent of wisteria filling the air. "Do you believe in magic?"

He shook his head before turning to her. "At least, I didn't."

"Hello," her father's voice called from further down the path.

"Hi, Dad."

"Afternoon, Mr Montgomery." Justin moved to release her hand but she squeezed it and held him still.

She didn't care if her dad saw them holding hands. Her father wouldn't mind her being with Justin. He was very open-minded about letting people love whoever they wanted and be whoever they wanted. Her mother was the same, and she was proud of their modern, unprejudiced views. If only more people were like them.

Besides, she already knew how much they liked Justin. After dinner, they hadn't stopped speaking his praises. Who wouldn't like Justin, after all? With his mild manners and easy conversation, he was just the sort of man most parents would be thrilled to welcome into a family.

"I would have thought you had gone back to Brisbane by now," Mark said. Although his gaze flickered over their intertwined fingers, he didn't mention it.

"I was packing things up when I got the call about your offer. I'm just doing due diligence."

"Not a problem. These things have to go through the right channels, after all. We're here when you're ready."

Justin smiled at Mark, and her father shook his hand warmly. "You should come over to the pub tonight. All the locals will be there for our regular Friday night dinner and trivia."

"Oh yeah, you must," Freya said enthusiastically. "It's parmy night at the Bunya Bar."

"Parmy?" He shot her a quizzical look.

"Parmigiana. You know, crumbed chicken schnitzel with cheese and tomato sauce. Fridays are pretty much Greer's only night off."

Mark nodded in agreement. "Even with all her experience, Greer still won't try to compete with the Bunya Bar when it comes to parmy night."

"Why would she want to give up her night off though, really." Freya adored her sister. She worked so hard and was so talented.

Justin chuckled. "I haven't had a good parmy in years."

"Great. I'll see you tonight then." Mark waved before turning down the path that led towards the milking shed, where the cows would be lining up ready for their afternoon milking.

Justin's gold-flecked hazel eyes held hers, and he spoke quietly. "Your family are great. I really like them."

Nerves skittered in her stomach. "Yeah, they are, and they like you too."

They continued up the path until Nutmeg came into view. She was quietly grazing in her paddock, just where Freya had left her that morning. "I was thinking that if you had grown up here, you probably would have learned how to ride a horse."

Justin looked at her with a furrowed brow. "Who says I don't know how to ride a horse?"

She rounded on him. "Do you?"

He laughed and shook his head. "No, I don't. But I know how to ride a bike, so it can't be that much harder, right?"

"Yeah, it's kind of different." She nodded before laughing. "Are you up to the challenge?"

He straightened. "Are you?"

She raised one eyebrow at him. "I am."

It didn't take long to saddle up Nutmeg, who dozed quietly as Freya tightened the girth and altered the stirrup length. After putting on the bridal, she handed Justin a helmet and waited for him to put it on.

"Okay, left foot in the stirrup and then lift yourself up," Freya said, turning the stirrup slightly, so he could angle his foot into it.

He tried but didn't get enough muscle behind the movement and ended up sliding back down the saddle, rather ungracefully.

She bit her lip so she wouldn't laugh at him. "That's okay—you've never done this before. Try again."

He repeated the process and this time managed to swing his leg up and over the back of the saddle. Before long he was sitting nervously astride her horse. She showed him how to hold the reins before gathering up the lead rope and urging the horse forward.

"Okay up there?" she asked when he remained silent.

"Yup."

Freya turned her neck and watched him. "Straighten your back and try to relax."

He did as she said, and after a few minutes he started to look more comfortable.

He looked good. Not just good—hot. She had always had a thing for guys on horseback.

Freya led Nutmeg around the paddock at an easy

gait. She could feel Justin's confidence growing with each step. "You're starting to get the hang of this."

"It's actually really fun. Beats mountain-bike riding—probably won't hurt as much tomorrow either."

"I don't know if that's true. If I go even a week without riding, I feel it the next day."

"Have you always liked horses?"

"Oh yeah. I was the kid who did pony club instead of ballet. I never competed seriously, but I loved being able to hang out with my best mate." She scratched Nutmeg behind the ear, just where the horse liked it. "Do you want to have a go by yourself?"

"Is that safe? Will you show me how?"

She nodded and unclipped the halter. "Nutmeg is as bombproof as they come. Finn rides her all the time."

She taught Justin how to direct and stop the horse before standing back and letting him practice. He caught on quickly, and the two walked around the paddock for quite a while.

She could see his mouth moving, and it occurred to her that he was talking to the horse. Horses, she found, were very therapeutic, and she wondered what he was saying. Was he talking about his father and the life he may have lived had his mother stayed? Was he talking about his life in Brisbane? Was he talking about her? Did he feel the same connection that she felt? Like they were meant to be?

Eventually, he pulled up alongside her and stopped. She searched his eyes for clues, but they were shaded over. Whatever he and Nutmeg had discussed was private.

He slid down slowly from the saddle, and together they untacked Nutmeg and brushed her down.

"Thanks for that." He stroked the horse's neck one more time.

She slipped her fingers into her back pockets, looking at him from under her lashes. "Did you really enjoy it?"

"Yeah, I really did. She's a beautiful horse."

Freya smiled proudly. "One of the perks of living in the country." She hugged the horse's neck and rubbed her cheek against the silky fur. She loved the smell of horse, even a sweaty one.

"I better go and get changed if I'm coming out to the pub for dinner tonight."

"And what exactly are you going to change into? I didn't think you had any spare clothes."

"I'll raid Boyd's closet again. Although it mostly consists of checked shirts and jeans."

"You probably wouldn't be my dad's size, otherwise I'd offer you some of his clothes." She looked Justin up and down. "His wardrobe is mostly checks and jeans too."

"Boyd's fit me fine. Thanks though."

She smiled as he handed her the helmet and their fingers brushed, causing heat to rush through her body. "Do you want me to walk you back to your car?"

"No, it's okay. I remember the way, and you probably have lots to do here."

She nodded, not wanting him to leave. "See you tonight then."

"Save me a seat?"

She nodded and watched as he turned and walked away. She would be happy to save him a seat next to her, every night for the rest of their lives.

CHAPTER 6

*J*ustin chose the nicest dress shirt he could find in his father's wardrobe and paired it with the least-faded jeans from the dresser. By the time he was ready to leave, he was twitching to see Freya again.

He couldn't stop thinking about her, the way she looked in the sunlight, her hands slid into her back pockets. How it made her breasts thrust against the thin fabric of her shirt and show the ridges of her lacy bra. The huskiness of her voice, the lowering of her eyes.

The Bunya Bar sat proudly on a rise overlooking the town. The double-storey Queenslander had a large balcony decorated with a variety of green hanging plants.

He followed the sound of music and laughter to

the bar where men dressed in high-vis shirts were nursing beers and chatting with their mates. Families and groups sat at tables in the adjoining dining room. He continued exploring the maze of rooms until he spotted Nina at an outside bar, ordering drinks.

"Justin, you made it. I'm so glad." She embraced him warmly. It was a mother's hug and reminded him of his own.

"I heard the parmy here was the best in Australia."

"It sure is, and the company's not too bad either. Now, what will you have?" She gestured to the bartender standing at the beer taps.

Justin ordered a locally brewed beer he had never heard of and chatted with Nina while they waited for their drinks.

"Freya said she took you to the factory today."

"Yes, those cheeses are amazing. Do you sell them anywhere in Brisbane?"

She grinned a smile so similar to her daughter's. "No, only on the Sunshine Coast at the moment, although Freya has big plans for Emerald Hills. She wants world domination."

"I bet."

She had the attitude and drive to achieve anything she set her mind to. It was one of the things he liked most about her.

Drinks in hand, he followed Nina to a large table outside surrounded by lush green bushes adorned with fairy lights.

He heard Freya laughing before he saw her, and when their eyes met, it was like everyone else melted into the background leaving just them together.

She waved him over, then stood and hugged him, kissing his cheek, igniting his skin in her wake. "I saved you a seat, just like I promised," she said, moving down the bench seat so he could sit next to her.

They sat close to each other, their arms and thighs touching. He took a gulp of beer, hoping it would numb his reaction to her. He was pleasantly surprised by the lager's fruity taste.

Nina raised her arms and demanded quiet as she introduced Justin to the table full of family and friends. Names were exchanged, and hands shaken, but it was hard to take it in with his brain full of Freya's scent and touch.

The man sitting on his left caught his attention and introduced himself as Shane. Justin shook his ring-adorned hand and tried not to stare at his long, dreadlocked beard which matched his long, dreadlocked hair.

"Are you enjoying Maleny?"

Justin nodded. "More than I expected. It's a great place."

"It is." Shane tipped his beer in Freya's direction. "And she's a great girl, so you better treat her right." Shane's voice broke into a chuckle ,and he slapped Justin on the back.

He could feel Freya's body heat drawing him in. His mouth went dry. When he looked over, she caught his glance, holding it with those amazing brown eyes of hers. The corners of her mouth curved just a little, causing thrilling tingles to course through his body.

Over deep conversations, they all ordered and ate their way through hearty servings of chicken parmigianas, salads, and hot, salty fries. By the time he was finished, Justin's stomach was full, and his sides were sore from laughter.

"How are you with trivia?" Freya leaned in close, and he caught a whiff of her perfume—a mixture of citrus and jasmine.

He gazed into her chocolate-coloured eyes and tried not to drown in their depths. "I'm okay. I do enjoy watching *Millionaire Hot Seat*."

She rubbed her hands together. "You can be on my team then."

They joined up with Greer and Mark, and spoke in huddled whispers as the trivia questions were called out.

"What's the capital of Brazil?"

"Rio de Janeiro?" Greer shrugged.

"No, it's Brasilia," Justin said. "Trust me," he added, when Freya looked at him suspiciously.

"Who won the 2014 FIFA world cup?"

Everyone turned to look at Justin. "I'm not really that into sport, but I would guess either Germany or France."

"What about England?" Freya asked.

"No, they haven't won in years," Mark replied.

Greer tapped her pen against the paper. "Which one?"

"France. No, Germany," Justin said.

Justin felt quietly confident when the questions were finished, and the answers were called out.

"Brasilia! You were right." Freya clapped him on the shoulder.

"The winner of the 2014 FIFA world cup was ... Germany."

"Wow, good job!"

In the end they only had two answers wrong, but still beat everyone else.

"What do we win?" he asked Freya.

"A meat tray." She laughed. "Just what you always wanted."

The publican carried over a huge tray full of sausages, steak and mince and laid it on the table.

"Barbeque at our place tomorrow?" Mark suggested.

"I hope that means the men are cooking." Greer crossed her arms but smiled good-naturedly.

Freya wrapped herself around Justin's arm. "It'll be fun."

"You're intent on keeping me up here, aren't you?"

"Is it working?" She fluttered her eyelashes.

How the hell was he supposed to resist when Freya looked at him like that? He had one hundred things he should have been doing back in Brisbane, but none of them appealed as much as being here with Freya. "I guess I could start packing up Boyd's things and go home Sunday."

"Yay." She kissed him ever so briefly on the lips and gazed into his eyes. "I'm not ready to let you go just yet."

CHAPTER 7

*J*ustin awoke to the distant mooing of cows and light shimmering into the room through the sheer old curtains. He had slept longer than he'd expected and felt refreshed and ready to face the day. Perhaps it was the clear Hinterland air. Whatever it was, he couldn't remember waking up feeling so good in a long time. If ever.

He climbed out of bed and practically skipped towards the kitchen, where he prepared himself a cup of coffee and a bowl of muesli before sitting out on the porch to eat his breakfast and watch the farm fully awaken.

He thought back on the night before, the people he had met and their seemingly easy way of life. Things up here seemed so much more relaxed and less chaotic than in the city. There was less pollution, less traffic, less noise, and less people.

How he would go back to his life now where he was always surrounded by strangers. He didn't even know the other residents in his apartment complex —everyone kept to themselves and minded their own business.

Here, everyone knew everyone and was always willing to lend a hand.

His father was still a mystery—however, his life made more sense now. This area was the only place he had ever lived. It had been his life even when his family had left.

Justin resolved to start sorting through boxes that weekend and see if he could find out anything more about the man who might as well have been a stranger. Perhaps answers to some mysteries would be uncovered. Perhaps he would just be left with more questions.

He finished off his cereal and coffee, cleaned up the dishes, then headed to the bathroom where he showered and dressed in more of his father's clothes.

He then opened the wooden doors of his father's closet, deciding it was as good a place as any to start. His father had been surprisingly tidy and didn't seem to own much of value.

Justin decided that if he put in a few long hours

he could easily have the job over and done with by the end of the weekend.

When he heard the sound of a car pull up on the gravel driveway, Justin stood and stretched. His morning sorting things hadn't uncovered anything he hadn't already known about his father.

Walking towards the front door, he hoped that like yesterday, Freya had decided to call in unannounced.

She had said last night she wasn't ready to let him go, and he realised he felt the same way. That was why it was so easy for him to stay in Maleny. Because she was here. Because she made him want more.

Opening the sliding door, he poked his head out and was surprised to see his half-sister. The teenager climbed out of her fiery-red hatchback and threw him a wide smile. She shut the door behind her and jogged up the short path to him.

"Felicity? What are you doing here?"

"I wanted to come and see what you'd inherited. Plus, I thought you might want a change of clothes."

Justin and his brother and sister all had spare keys to each other's houses in case of emergencies.

Felicity often turned up, unannounced, to crash on his couch when she needed a break from their parents.

"You brought clothes?" Finally, he'd be able to get out of the farm shirts and workwear that still had a faint smell of milk and manure—despite the heavy-duty washing. "Thank you. What about my razor?" He rubbed a hand along his jaw, feeling the rasp of stubble against his palm.

"Oops, sorry." Felicity shrugged. "But I like this look on you." She gestured to his face, then stepped backwards, and put her hands on her hips, taking in the plainness of the cottage. "Okay, I admit: I was expecting more."

"Just wait until you see inside." He opened the door wide and waved her in.

He boiled the kettle and brewed a fresh pot of coffee while she made herself at home and inspected the small house. Coming back, from her inspection, she sat in a chair and accepted her mug.

"So, what do you think?" he asked, as he sat next to her at the table.

"Well it could be worse. But it could also be better."

"I don't plan on keeping it."

"No. I can't imagine you as a dairy farmer. But

there are plenty of other things you could do up here."

"Yeah? Like what?"

"You run your own business; you could do that anywhere. You don't have to be in Brisbane. In fact, I bet you would save a lot of money living up here, not having to pay that huge rent for your apartment in the city."

"The apartment you enjoy crashing at most Saturday nights." He waggled his brows at her.

She shrugged nonchalantly. "So, have you got a buyer for it yet?"

Justin sipped his coffee. "The neighbours next door want to lease it out. I'm just waiting for final approvals before I sign the forms."

"Lease? Wouldn't it be better to sell it and get rid of it, maybe use the money to buy something"—she looked around at the peeling wallpaper—"a bit more modern? Something redecorated in the last thirty years."

"I can lease it out to these guys, and then hope a sale comes up at some stage."

Felicity nodded. "Well, I saw it has a spare room."

"You want to stay the night? Here?"

"Might as well bludge off you while I can," she teased.

"You do that back home anyway."

As they were finishing catching up on each other's news, Justin saw an unfamiliar white hatchback rolling down the driveway.

"Expecting someone?" Felicity asked as she followed his gaze.

His eyes widened as he recognised the familiar face. Freya climbed out of the car with a plastic container under her arm.

Justin felt his sister's gaze upon him.

"Good morning." Freya was only a few steps away and he felt the sparks between them as she watched him. Her face fell when she spotted Felicity.

"Freya, this is my sister, Felicity." He watched as Freya looked from him to Felicity as though searching for familial resemblance then, seeming satisfied, she turned to the younger woman with a wide smile.

"So, you're Justin's sister. I'm so glad to meet you." Her voice was warm.

Felicity, who never missed a trick, was also appraising the newcomer. "Great to meet you too," she said, and leaned in for a friendly hug.

It suddenly occurred to Justin just how much these two would have in common. They were bound to be kindred spirits, both women having bubbly personalities and positive attitudes.

"I come bearing gifts," Freya said, holding out the

plastic container. "I have sustenance from Greer. And boxes."

"Boxes?" Felicity raised an eyebrow.

"Packing boxes—we're into recycling over at Emerald Hills. Hardly anything ever gets thrown out, which means our shed is full of just about everything you could possibly imagine. Since you're packing up Boyd's things, you're going to need these."

Freya and Felicity chatted like they had known each other all their lives while they got the boxes out, taped them up, and then they all started to pack room by room.

Although not always participating in the conversation, Justin listened with an avid ear, picking up on things he hadn't known about Freya or indeed his sister.

They talked in depth about the latest social media trends, a big part of Freya's business.

"We should totally take a selfie," Felicity exclaimed, grabbing her phone and waving Justin over to join them. With a pile of boxes for their backdrop, Felicity held the camera at arm's length. "Come on, you two. Get a bit closer."

Justin found himself squeezed between the two young women. He watched the phone screen as Freya tucked her head into the curve of his neck and felt the electricity fire through his body from being so close to her.

Felicity snapped a few photos before looking through them.

Justin turned to Freya, who smiled adoringly back at him. God, she was so beautiful. "Thanks for helping."

"Of course, happy to. Although I was hoping you could help me with something later."

He looked at her with a furrowed brow. "What exactly did you need help with?"

"The website. It's been driving me nuts, and you're an IT expert."

"Oh, okay. What do you need help with?"

"It'll be easier if I show you. I have my laptop in the car. We can do it later."

"I hope it's okay if I tag you two this photo?" Felicity said. "And Freya, I've just sent you a friend request."

Freya slid her mobile from the back pocket of her jeans. A few taps later, she declared it done. She glanced at Justin. "I just sent you one too."

He joined the party and pulled out his own mobile, swiping away all the unread messages and emails he would have to deal with eventually. Logging into his Facebook account, he accepted

Freya's request, and couldn't help but quickly scroll through her profile.

Pictures of her around the farm, and around Maleny, filled her feed. Her natural beauty was emphasised even more by the green and brown hues of the Hinterland. There were other photos too, selfies of her with other people, laughing and obviously enjoying themselves.

He couldn't help but feel jealous whenever another man appeared in the pictures. He paused when he recognised the man with dreadlocks from Friday night. They seemed awfully close in the picture, one arm casually tossed around her shoulder, and their faces touching.

"Isn't that Shane from the other night?" He showed the picture to Freya.

"Yeah. We dated the last year of high school, before he turned vegan and got dreadlocks." She shrugged off the comment, as though it didn't mean anything.

"I thought you guys were just friends." He fought to keep his voice casual.

"We are friends. We both grew up in Maleny and have known each other since childhood. We couldn't give that up just because it didn't work out between us."

"Wow, I could never stay friends with an ex," Felicity said. "Too much water under the bridge."

"This is a small town. If we didn't stay friends with our exes, we wouldn't have many friends at all."

The three of them went back to their work, but it suddenly bothered Justin that so many of the men he met around town, that were roughly their age, could have been men Freya dated. They could have been people she'd considered being with long-term. She could have even loved some of them.

It made him feel insecure and jealous. Two feelings he had very little experience with. He wondered about the past; why had Freya and Shane broken up? Why would anyone let Freya go when she was such an amazing person?

He really liked Freya. He more than just liked her. He really, really, really liked her. She was the sort of girl he wanted to change his Facebook setting to 'in a relationship' with.

"Are you going to take this back for Mum?" Felicity said holding a wedding photo of his parents.

He recognised it and shook his head. "She already has the exact one."

Shit, what was he thinking? She was a country girl; he was a city boy. As much as he really wanted a relationship with her, it wouldn't work. Would it?

"Oh my God, you are a lifesaver." Freya clapped her hands and looked down at Justin.

After a delicious lunch courtesy of Greer, Justin had offered to fix Freya's website.

"You just accomplished in ten minutes what I've been trying to do for two and a half weeks."

He swivelled his chair and looked proudly at her. "It was nothing," he said humbly, but she knew it was a lie.

If it was easy, she would have worked it out. She knew her way around most technological aspects of the website and knew where to go for help, but this particular HTML code had been doing her head in.

"No, seriously, you know what you're doing, and I don't know how to thank you for that." She placed both her hands on either side of his face and pressed a kiss to his lips.

It had meant to be a fun 'thank you' kiss, but as she pulled away from his mouth, and gazed into his eyes, she knew he wanted more. Just like she wanted more.

"Freya." Her name was barely a whisper on his lips.

Her gaze darted to his mouth and back. She swallowed, lost in his hazel-coloured eyes.

Her laptop pinged, breaking the moment. She averted her gaze towards it and dropped her hands.

Justin turned in his chair and cleared his throat.

Noting it was just an incoming email, and nothing she needed to deal with straight away, she closed her laptop and tucked it under her arm. "I'm serious. I really appreciate that."

"Anytime." He smiled back at her. The impulse to grab him close and taste those lips again was strong.

Felicity chose that moment to walk in on them sitting at the dining room table. "I just taped up the last box."

"We have more," Freya said. "I can bring them over tomorrow." She was happy for any excuse to come back and continue where they had left off.

"Another day packing? Can't we do something fun tomorrow?" Felicity slumped into the couch, looking tired and worn out.

"We'll talk about it tomorrow." Justin stood from the table and glanced at the clock on the wall. "We better get ready for tonight's barbecue."

Felicity sat up straighter, a smile spreading across her face. "Barbecue? What barbecue?"

Freya grinned at her new friend, thrilled that Justin's younger sister was such a fun, outgoing girl. The sort of girl Freya enjoyed hanging out with and chatting to.

"We won the meat tray at the pub last night, so we're having a barbecue at our house," Freya said.

"I can't wait to meet the rest of your family." Felicity had been asking questions about Greer and her parents all day, and about Emerald Hills and how Freya was building their social media presence.

"There will be more than just my family there," Freya turned to Justin. . "Mum was inviting a few of our friends; so many people want to meet you."

The main reason they wanted to meet him was because he was Boyd's son. The elusive offspring they had forgotten even existed. Being new was a novelty in town, and even though the gossip line was very active in Maleny, people always wanted first-hand reports. The fact that he was young, fresh blood, would also make him the favourite subject with any parents of eligible young women. Not to mention the young women themselves, who were always on the lookout for love.

Freya knew she would have to stay close to Justin tonight. If anyone was going to win his heart, it would be her. She squirmed inwardly. She couldn't stand the idea of him being with one of her school-mates. Not when the attraction between them was so strong.

She thought back to earlier, when he had been checking out her Facebook page and had come across that photo of her and Shane. She was sure it had been jealousy flickering across his face.

And tomorrow he planned on leaving.

Unless she gave him a reason to stay, or at the very least, to come back.

reya had expected her mother to invite a lot of people, but as they walked around to the back of the house, it looked like at least half the town had turned up.

"The meat tray was big," Justin said just loudly enough for her to hear, "but it wasn't that big."

She brushed his arm with her own, unable to avoid touching him for more than a few minutes. The look he shot her told her that he felt the same.

"Wow, this place is great," Felicity exclaimed beside her. "Justin, if you'd inherited a place like this, there is no way I'd let you give it up."

He chuckled at his sister's enthusiasm.

"There's Greer. I'll introduce you." Freya led them towards her sister and introduced Felicity.

"Freya told me you're an amazing chef. I love

cooking, but I don't think I'm very good at it," Felicity said.

"I spent so many years studying and travelling. I've worked in restaurants in lots of different cities, trying the local dishes and learning about the produce. I'd be happy to help you out if you're ever interested in learning more," Greer said kindly.

"I'd love that." Felicity beamed at Greer.

Where Justin was reserved and introverted, Felicity was assertive and self-confident but his love for his sister was evident in the proud smiles he bestowed on her.

Mark joined them, handing Justin a bottle of beer. "How did the packing go today?"

Justin's reply was polite and friendly as usual. "I got a lot done, thanks to these helpers." He motioned to Freya and Felicity. "Thanks for the boxes."

"That was all Freya; she knows where everything is around this place," her father replied. "If I can steal you away from these lovely ladies, there are some people who would like to meet you."

Justin turned and glanced at Freya, as though hoping for a cue as to his next move. She gave him her permission with a smile and nod.

For a few seconds, he held her stare, before breaking away to follow her father.

"He'll be okay." Greer leaned in close. "You can't have them all to yourself, all the time."

Freya was about to admonish her sister for saying such things in front of Felicity when she realised Felicity wasn't there anymore. She glanced around anxiously.

Greer gestured to where Justin's sister was now talking animatedly to Nina. "That Felicity is quite a character."

"She sure is. Certainly less reserved than her brother."

"You really like him."

Freya felt her cheeks reddening. "Is it that obvious?"

"It is to me. Then again, I know you better than anyone."

"I've never felt like this before."

"Really? Ever?"

"No. This time it's different."

"He seems very nice. Genuine. I just don't want you to get your heart broken when he goes back to the city."

"I know, but Brisbane's not that far. Maybe it could work."

Greer shrugged. "I do think he's attracted to you. I mean, look at the way he keeps glancing over here."

Freya turned towards him and their eyes

connected. It was only for a moment, but it felt significant.

"You know I'll always tell you to follow your heart. If you can find someone you want to be with, then that's great, and you should try to make it work."

"It's not too late for you, Greer. You'll find someone." Freya hugged her sister and sent up a silent prayer that she would find happiness soon.

"I know. I just hope that when I finally meet the man of my dreams my ovaries won't have shrunken entirely. Did you know a woman's fertility decreases significantly after the age of twenty-eight?"

"No. But thanks for the biology lesson. Now I need a drink. What about you?"

Greer shook her head and disappeared to restock the cheese platters.

With no sun left, the air temperature was dropping fast, the cold tickling her lungs. Freya headed over to a table full of beer bottles, wine, and a various array of premixed spirits. She chose a can of Coke and opened the top. Seeing Justin still deep in conversation with her father, she decided to leave them to it. She wandered around the edge of the group and found her favourite spot. A large fig tree sat at the top of an incline, which had a beautiful view of the sloping hills. Many years ago, her father had built a bench seat, so people could sit and take in the landscape. She sat there now and breathed in deeply, savouring the cool night air.

With the chatter of the guests creating a back-drop, she leaned back in the chair, and let her thoughts return to Justin. Her skin goose pimpled as she thought of all the things she wanted to do to him, how much she wanted his touch on her skin, his lips on her mouth. Just thinking about the way he stood talking to her father made her want him.

Everything about him made her want him.

As if he had been summoned by the force of her thoughts, he appeared next to her. "Mind if I sit next to you?" His voice was full of something—desire?

"Please do."

He sat next to her. Closer than he needed to. Close enough to touch.

"You and my father were talking for a while."

He sipped his beer before looking at her. "He's a great guy. I didn't think we would have much in common, but we really do."

She smiled. "He has a way of finding things in common with everyone."

"I wanted to thank you for everything you've done for me. If it wasn't for you, I would have gone home by now. I hadn't even planned on coming up for the funeral, but I'm so glad I did. Not only have I learnt more about Boyd, but I also got to meet so many unique people. And I'm so thankful to you, and your family, for your generosity and kindness."

His words were so heartfelt, and said with such passion, she felt her eyes moisten. "You don't have to thank us. We like you; we want to help you."

"You like me?" He raised a brow and his mouth curved up.

She felt her pulse quicken and her mouth go dry.

She started to speak but he silenced her, covering her mouth with his.

Fireworks shot through her veins the moment their lips connected. The heat of his body, his arms around her. She parted her lips for him, angling her head and letting him take the kiss deep.

She had never been kissed like this before. By a man who acted like he was starving for her. And she had never felt like she was starving for a man before either. It was completely intoxicating.

When they finally broke apart for air, he brushed a light kiss on her lips and dropped his hands.

"I've been wanting to do that for a while," he breathed into her hair.

Desire quivered in her stomach. "Me too."

She turned toward him again and rubbed her hand over his rough cheek, then lowered her mouth to his. Her hands explored his chest and arms while her tongue explored his mouth. She couldn't get enough. She wanted him. All of him.

And he wanted her. She could feel his desire as he pulled her against him. He groaned as though reading her thoughts.

"We should go back to the party." His voice was deep, smooth, and so damned sexy.

"They won't miss us," she murmured, not wanting the moment to end.

"Freya, I want you more than you can possibly imagine. But this is neither the time or place He disentangled himself and looked her in the eyes. "I want our first time to be special. And I don't want to risk being interrupted." The certainty of his tone was almost her undoing.

She would have been perfectly happy making love to him on top of a hay bale in the shed, but she appreciated him wanting to take it slow.

He kissed her again, nibbling gently on her lip, before lifting her up and placing her on her feet. "Let's go get some food before it's all gone," he said, and took her hand in his.

CHAPTER 9

*J*ustin woke with thoughts of Freya swelling in his mind. Last night, he had finally held her in his arms and tasted that sweet, sweet mouth. If only he didn't want more now. If only a kiss had been enough. If only it hadn't made him want her even more. He would have been able to go back to the city and forget about her. Instead it had only cemented their attraction towards each other. Proved that what it was between them was truly magical.

Freya was not forgettable. He knew for the rest of his life he would never forget her or that kiss. And he had a gut feeling that if he left now, he would regret it forever.

The sun shone brilliantly through the curtains, enticing him out of bed. He dressed in his own clothes. He wore a pair of denim jeans and a T-shirt, finding a wool jumper to go over it. After putting on shoes and socks, he headed for the kitchen, knowing his sister would appreciate a fresh cup of coffee as much as he would.

He was surprised to find Felicity, coffee in hand, in his usual spot on the deck. "Since when do you get up before ten on the weekend?"

Felicity turned and smiled. "How could you possibly sleep through a sunrise here? It was so spectacular. It really makes you think about things."

"And what do you have to think about these days?" he asked his sister. He remembered high school well enough; he knew the stress that fitting in and achieving academically could put on kids. Felicity was mature for her age and, as far as he knew, doing well in her last year of school, even with looming exams.

"Why would you want to go back to Brisbane when you could be here?" She gestured to the land in front of her, and he turned his attention to the rolling hills and the grazing black and white cattle.

"This coming from the city girl?"

"I'm only a city girl because that's the way I was raised."

"I was raised that way too,"

"It wasn't always that way. At least you got four

years out here before you moved to the city."

"They were four years I don't even remember."

"Can you imagine your life here though? Starting now? With Freya?"

He turned to his sister, his mouth open.

Her eyes glittered, and a sly smile tilted the corner of her mouth. "I see the way you two are together—you're in love with her."

He sighed and sank into the chair next to his sister. He knew he couldn't deny his feelings for Freya. "It would mean uprooting my entire life. Starting again."

"There's nothing wrong with starting again—not if it means you're going to live a better life. Don't you think she's worth it?"

Justin sighed. Of course, these were the same questions swirling around in his own mind. But he had only known Freya a short time and it was too soon to make such drastic life changes with a woman he'd only just met. Despite the fact his whole body was telling him she was the one for him—the one he'd been waiting his whole life for.

"These are very deep questions to be asking a man who hasn't even had coffee yet." He stood and started towards the door.

She stopped him. "Justin, can we do something fun today?"

"What kind of fun?"

"This is the Sunshine Coast; Noosa is just up the road."

He couldn't deny the twinkle in her eye. She was his baby sister. The spoilt but angelic child who, almost always, got her way. "Noosa as in Hastings Street, people watching and expensive shops?" He frowned; it didn't exactly seem like his sister's scene.

"Noosa as in the beach. One of Queensland's best beaches."

Justin chuckled at his sister. How long had it been since he had been to a beach? Since he'd felt sand under his feet?

"I am sure Freya could drive us there. I'll text her now and see."

He groaned as he watched Felicity pick up her phone and start tapping on the screen. Once his sister had an idea in her head, there was no denying her. Besides, a day at the beach could be just what they all needed: a change of scenery, and some sun and warmth.

Before he knew it, Justin was sitting in the passenger side of Freya's hatchback driving down the range towards the coast. Felicity sat in the middle of the back seat, chatting endlessly to her new-found friend about the countryside, and what it was like growing up in the Hinterland.

Justin listened to the women, and replied when asked questions, but spent most of his time gazing at the amazing scenery around him.

"That's the Baroon Dam you can see to the left," Freya said, and Justin caught a glimpse of the large lake down in a gully, surrounded by huge mountains.

"Can you fish in there?" he asked.

"You can, but you need a permit. You can also stand-up paddleboard, kayak, canoe, and do all sorts of adventurous things."

They drove through the busy tourist town of Montville, before heading into even quieter countryside.

Justin turned to watch Freya and was struck again by her beauty, the soft lines of her, the way her skin was perfectly sun-kissed.

When they finally reached the bustling seaside town of Noosa, Freya found a parking spot and they all climbed out of the car, happy to stretch their legs after an hour of sitting.

"Too bad we didn't bring swimsuits," Justin said, eyeing off the sign directing them to the beach.

"Never fear," Felicity said, as she pulled a bag

from the back seat. "I packed some just in case."

"You brought my swimsuit from the city?" He looked at his sister in surprise.

"It's the Sunshine Coast—the chance we were going to swim was always high."

Justin turned to Freya. "Did you bring yours?"

"Of course. You can't come to Noosa without swimming."

"But it's the middle of winter."

"And it's Queensland."

He couldn't deny it was warm; he'd already taken off his jumper.

Freya was wearing a summer dress that revealed bare shoulders. She led the way down a path surrounded by bush, until they emerged on the white silky sands of the Noosa foreshore. The bay curved gently, flat golden sand leading out to the calm waters bobbing with sailboats. They could hear the distant honk of the ferry.

They found an empty stretch of sand between sunbathers and set up their things then took turns going to the change rooms and switching outfits to their bathing suits. Justin looked out across the ocean and breathed in the warm, salty air.

Justin was grateful that his sister had packed his board shorts. The pull of the ocean was strong, and he couldn't wait to see Freya in a bikini.

And he wasn't disappointed. She came back with her hair in a high topknot, wearing a navy-blue bikini which left little to the imagination. She was confident with her body, making her even more attractive to him.

Before long they were running to the water's edge and splashing in the cool water.

"Do you come to the beach often?" he asked Freya.

"Not as often as I'd like. I keep forgetting we have such a gem so close by."

"If I lived here, I'd come to the beach all the time," Felicity exclaimed before diving into a wave and emerging on the other side.

Justin swam closer to Freya so that they were both at neck-level in water. With Felicity entertaining herself in the deeper waves, he reached out his hands and placed them on Freya's hips, drawing her closer. She leaned in and kissed him; she tasted salty and delicious.

Freya groaned in his arms and pressed her body against his. He moved his hands over her bare skin, fighting the urge to take her right there and then.

"You drive me crazy," he murmured when they finally pulled apart.

"The feeling is mutual," she said before slipping from his arms and diving under the water. He chased her for a while before they decided to join Felicity farther out.

When they finally tired of the water, they walked back to their towels, and lay on the sand. He was surprised the beach wasn't more populated. A few families played, children built sandcastles, while pale bodies sunbathed and read books.

"I know a great place we should go for lunch," Freya suggested.

"I'm starving," Felicity said as she put her T-shirt and shorts on over the top of her swimsuit. "But I want to go shopping first. Can I meet you there?"

Freya gave Felicity the address and they waved her off. Then Freya curled up next to Justin.

He put his arm under her head and held her. The feeling of her beside him felt so natural and perfect.

"This feels so right, doesn't?" she said.

"I was just thinking the same thing."

Freya lifted her head, putting her chin on his chest. "Do you think we could try and make this work?"

"Are you sure you want to? Long-distance relationships can be hard."

"I'm willing to do whatever we have to do." She kissed his chest and moved her hand provocatively across his chest.

He groaned and rolled her on top of him,

bringing her mouth to his, wanting her, needing her so much it hurt.

"When does Felicity go home?" Freya asked.

"Tonight."

She raised an eyebrow at him. "So you'll have the house to yourself?"

"Seems I will." He kissed her forehead

"Will you come over? Will you spend the night with me, Freya?"

She smiled and nodded. "I will."

He rolled her over so she was on her back and he could keep kissing her as deeply as he needed to. His kisses were full of the promise of what lay ahead that night. The pleasure he would give her. The love he would show her.

They met Felicity at a funky little café just off Hastings Street.

Over a delicious lunch of pasta and salads, they chatted about their childhood and laughed. Justin couldn't remember the last time he had laughed so much. When their stomachs were full to bursting, they decided to head back up the range.

Justin couldn't help but keep checking his watch; the sooner they got back, the sooner Felicity would leave, the sooner Freya could come over and the lovemaking could begin.

Freya must have felt it too. She kept sliding him glances and suggestive looks.

"Are you coming back to the city soon?" Felicity asked later as she packed the car, ready to go.

"We'll see. I've got my laptop, and I'm doing some work when I can."

Freya had left after hugging Felicity and promising that they would see each other again soon.

"I really like her," Felicity said to her brother as she prepared to head home. "Her mum and dad too. She is perfect for you."

"Thanks, sis."

He watched his sister drive away as the sun set over the mountains. A cool wind blew through the paddocks and he hugged himself. How would he feel when it came time to leave?

He went back inside the house and cleaned up in anticipation of Freya's arrival. Boxes were stacked in most rooms of the house now. His father's clothes and knick-knacks were ready for transporting, but he still didn't know where they would go. He hadn't found anything he wanted to take back with him. As he sat on the couch, feeling happy that it was now an estate worthy of

Freya visit, he noticed the coffee table had a drawer.

How have I not noticed this before?

He bent over and slid it open; a large leather-bound photo album took up the entire drawer. He pulled it out and leafed through it.

Faded photographs of his parents, and him as a child, filled the pages, and he felt tears sting his eyes. It looked well-loved, as though his father had flipped through them many times over the years. A picture of him as a toddler was the final photo in the book. The last image his father had of him. There were only blank pages after that. Gaps that should have been filled with shots of him growing up, but instead they were empty.

He wondered again why his father hadn't fought for him. Why he had never tried to contact him. Grief slammed into him for the first time. He and his father had missed a life together. He had missed getting to know his father and his father had missed getting to know him. He would never know the reason why they had missed the opportunity to be together and he swore silently. He would never know the real reason they had been apart, he swore silently to himself that he would never give up an opportunity to share his life with anyone he loved.

Including Freya.

CHAPTER 10

Freya tapped lightly on the screen door. She could see Justin sitting in the living room, hunched over something. He looked up to her and she saw his eyes were red and puffy. Without hesitating, she opened the door and stepped inside. Within seconds she was beside him, gathering him into her arms and stroking his hair. She whispered reassurances in his ear.

His arms enveloped her. His hands roamed over her back and she felt herself tingle under his touch. He nuzzled his way up to her mouth where his lips met hers, hot and hungry, in a searing kiss that shot all the way to her fingers and toes.

He broke the kiss and drew back to look at her. "Are you sure about this?"

She wrapped her arms around his neck and pressed against him. "You're kidding, right?"

"No. I'm serious. I need to know."

She pressed her lips against his and even though the contact was brief, she shivered at the restrained desire sizzling in the coiled strength of his hard body. "Yes. I want you."

As soon as the words were out of her mouth, he picked her up and carried her to the bedroom, laying her down on the bed. She pulled him on top of her, his deliciously aroused body pressed against her in all the right places.

She kissed along his spiky jawline and farther down to the soft skin of his neck. His pulse throbbed against her roaming lips.

He straightened and pulled off his shirt, revealing his toned torso with a smattering of fine, brown hair. She reached up to run her palms over his body and he groaned before reaching for her T-shirt and tugging it up.

As she rid herself of her clothes, he pulled off his jeans, all the while watching her. She lay back on the bed and he sat beside her. He slowly moved his focus from her face to scan her body, hovering on her breasts and slipping lower. His lips parted as his expression glazed over with increasing desire.

This time, he didn't hold back. He kissed her

deeply, probing her warm mouth as her body arched up against him, her tongue sliding to match his own wet strokes. It was incredible, the heat igniting him deep inside.

He rolled on a condom, and then he was with her, settling between her thighs—where he belonged.

Oh God. She thought she'd felt pleasure before, but this was something else. He was surging inside her, stroking her so deep, she was losing her mind. Freya clung onto him, rising to meet every thrust, until they were moving as one, each new stroke driving her higher, setting her blood on fire.

There were no words left, just the feel of him— hard, and deep, and so damn right she never wanted it to end. But her body couldn't hold back. Soon, she was cresting, right there on the edge, his body bearing down on her and his mouth claiming hers.

Freya gave up trying to process the sensations crashing through her. She laid back and revelled in the waves of incredible pleasure.

Nothing compared to the ecstasy he brought her. Physical, emotional, total. This wasn't just sex—this was a level of intimacy she'd never experienced before. Love in its most intense form.

Justin woke in the most blissful state to see that dawn was breaking outside. Freya was draped over him, half tangled up in the sheets. She was everything he'd fantasised about and more. And to have her ... finally. Like this. Like he had wanted from the moment he had laid eyes on her ...

It was more than intoxicating.

She opened those big brown eyes of hers and smiled up at him.

"Good morning," he whispered, his finger lightly tracing patterns across her collarbone.

"Morning, yourself."

Her phone chimed from the living room where she had happily forgotten it the night before. "What time is it?"

He twisted his head to see the digital clock on the bedside table. "Just after six."

She stretched. "I haven't slept this late in years."

He chuckled. "You call this late?"

She kissed his chin. "It is when you live on a dairy farm. Dad will have been up since four."

Justin's thoughts turned to Boyd, and he tried to swallow down the emotion.

"He would have been proud of you." Freya stroked the hair around his ear. "I'm sure he loved you and just wanted you to be happy."

"Is that why he never wrote to me? Never came

to visit me?" His voice was full of venom, not directed at her—he hoped she knew that. "Did he think I'd be happier without him in my life?"

Freya rolled onto her side and ran her fingers over his chest. "Maybe he didn't want to be a distraction. Maybe he thought you were better off without him."

He closed his eyes. "I was happy without him. I had my stepdad, and he was great. But now I realise that I'll never have the opportunity to know Boyd, my real father. I'm so angry with him, because he never gave me the chance to know him."

She softly wiped away the single tear that rolled down his cheek. "You did miss out. But he missed out on knowing you and that was the greater loss." She kissed his cheek, then looked him in the eye. "I wouldn't give up knowing you for anything."

He saw the sincerity of her words, the honesty and empathy with which she lived her life.

She slipped her arm around him and rested her head against his chest. Justin lay back, feeling her body rise and fall with every breath.

An unfamiliar sense of peace swept over him.

"Stay." After having made love to her again, Justin leaned across the bed, and pulled Freya in for another kiss.

"I can't. I have to go to work." She gave him a longing look before pulling on her jeans.

He admired the way they clung to her thighs and backside. Her body was perfect, and his fingers itched to discover it again and again and again.

And God, it felt right. Perfectly, wonderfully right.

He threw back the sheet covers and pulled on his jeans before following her to the living room. The air was cold against his shirtless chest and he shivered.

"It's been raining," she said from the window. Outside, low clouds blanketed the fields. "The mist should rise soon. We need the rain though, so we can't complain."

He went to her and touched her shoulder, letting his hand glide down her arm until their fingers linked. He brought her palm to his mouth and placed a gentle kiss against it. "When can I see you again?"

Her smile lit up her face as though she had been hoping he would ask just that question. "How about lunch? You can come to the café, or we can try somewhere else?"

"Only if I can have you for dessert," he teased as he pulled her in for another heart-stopping kiss.

"I'm sure that can be arranged." She held him close against her for a moment before letting go, gathering her belongings, and slipping out the door.

He leaned against the doorframe and watched her drive away. He could still smell her intoxicating scent in the room, on himself.

He was so grateful for having met Freya. This amazing, sexy woman who seemed to understand him and know him like no one else.

Shit.

Falling in love with her wasn't on the agenda. Though as his heart continued to thump and his skin tingled at the memory of her touch, he had the uneasy feeling it was already too late.

Shaking his head, he walked back to the bedroom where he showered and shaved. He was making the bed when his phone rang. He answered the call and greeted his lawyer.

"I've got some news, Justin. We've had an enquiry about the farm, from a solicitor acting on behalf of a property developer." The lawyer paused dramatically. "They have made an offer."

Justin's head was spinning. Faced with the chance to sell, he realised he'd been leaning towards leasing the estate out to the Montgomerys after all. *When did that happen?*

"What does a developer want with a dairy farm?"

"They want to turn it into a housing estate."

Justin heard the hesitation in the lawyer's voice. *A housing estate.* All Justin could picture were cookie-cutter houses crammed onto tiny blocks of land. His father's farm would be carved up into little chunks and sold off for top dollar.

The idea didn't sit well with him, but he also had to think about himself and his future. He had to at least consider this.

"What kind of an offer are we talking about?"

"A very generous amount. I think you should come into the office."

reya drove straight to the café and parked in the staff parking. She didn't want her mum or dad to pick up on her post-coital glow and tease her about being out all night.

She wanted to keep her budding new relationship with Justin private—for a little while longer at least. She wanted to revel in their love bubble as long as she could without having to think about what might happen tomorrow.

The café was bustling with the breakfast crowd. Tourists often came up for a hearty meal of bacon and eggs or pancakes before touring the working dairy farm.

The guides were as entertaining as they were informative, and guests were often so happy by the end of the tour that they'd stop by the shop and fill a cooler bag or two of Emerald Hills produce. They'd buy milk, yogurt and cheese to take away with them, and share the stories and experiences they'd enjoyed with their family and friends.

Freya made her way to her office, a small little room near the kitchen, where she shut the door and opened her laptop. She had advertising campaigns to review, videos to edit, and media releases to send off. All the jobs she should get done, instead of daydreaming about Justin and their incredible lovemaking.

She was roused two hours later by a rapping on the door and looked up as Greer walked in with a steaming cup of coffee.

"Good morning." Greer gave her a wink and handed her the cup, which Freya sipped gratefully.

"Thank you. I really needed a caffeine hit."

Greer sank into the couch opposite. "Late night?" She quirked an eyebrow at her sister.

Freya peeked at her from behind the cup while trying to hide her smile.

"That good, huh?"

Freya nodded. The idea of spending every night in Justin's bed—sharing life's delights and challenges —took root.

"I'm so jealous. I miss being in love." Greer's voice was lined with despair. She hid it well, but Freya knew her sister better than anyone. "So, when are you going to see him again?"

"We're meeting for lunch."

"Overnight visits, then a lunch date? It's getting serious."

"Hopefully." Freya's phone pinged beside her and she smiled when she saw Justin's name on the screen.

Her expression fell, and her stomach clenched, as she read his message.

"Is that him? What's wrong?" Greer asked.

"He has to cancel lunch. Apparently, he's got a meeting with his lawyer."

"Maybe they're working on the lease agreement. I know how keen Dad is to take it on."

Freya hoped that was the reason. It would be great for Emerald Hills to run Boyd's farm—hell, it would be great for Maleny. Keeping farms in the community meant keeping local jobs and opportunities. Plus, Justin would still have a link to them—a reason to visit and check in on things.

But her gut told her it was something else. "I have a bad feeling."

"I'm sure it will be okay." Her sister walked around the desk and hugged her. "He'll probably call you later with good news."

Freya smiled at her, hoping she was right.

Greer headed back to the kitchen to prepare for the lunch rush, and Freya tried to concentrate on her work. The potential for disappointment and the niggling sensation that something was wrong kept her preoccupied.

What if he was having second thoughts? Or regretted their night together?

What if he was one of those guys who lost interest in a girl after sleeping with them?

She didn't think he was that kind of man. Nothing he had said or done had made her think he was anything less than honourable. Normally she was a good judge of character and could tell if a person was being honest or not.

She had always had such a good feeling about Justin.

Why did he suddenly need to meet with his lawyer? Especially when he had been so eager to be with her that morning? Surely the leasing paper-work could wait.

What could possibly have changed?

Justin's heart and head pounded as he drove up the dirt driveway to the Montgomerys' house. Pulling up next to Freya's car, he was greeted by Denver. As he closed the car door, he bent down and scratched the dog's head, hoping he would receive as friendly a greeting from the residents inside.

The door swung open, and he looked up to see Freya standing in the outline of the doorway, the light from inside shining around her silhouette, throwing a dark shadow across her face. He took his time climbing the stairs, practising what he would say in his mind.

"This is a nice surprise." Freya reached for him and he moved into her embrace. He held her tightly, breathing in the scent that was so perfectly her.

He wanted this. He wanted her, but the news he brought could change everything. What would she say? How would they all react? His chest tightened uncomfortably.

After a long time, he pulled back. "Is your father home?"

She nodded and looked at him with questioning eyes. "What's wrong, Justin?"

"I have news. News I need to tell all of you."

He watched as she swallowed, then held the door open for him to come in.

Her father greeted him with his usual friendly handshake and waved him onto the couch. They sat and exchanged niceties while Freya rounded up her sister and mother.

Justin declined the drink Mark offered, thinking once they heard his news, they may not want him to stay.

"Well, don't keep us in suspense," Nina said when they were all gathered.

Justin took a deep breath before sharing his news. "I spent today with someone who has made an offer to buy Boyd's farm."

He was met with raised eyebrows and open mouths. He continued, "It's a property developer from Noosa. They are very interested in buying it."

The silence was deafening. He could see their faces falling as though this was the worst news they could have received.

"I appreciate you telling us this," said Mark. "Are you going to accept the offer?"

"There are still some details to be looked at before they can finalise the offer, so I honestly don't know. But I wanted to be honest and open with all of you. From my perspective, it would be easier for me to sell the farm and use the money to invest and help my family."

"But a property developer—they'll turn it into a housing estate." Freya's voice was quiet but serious.

"The region is growing, Freya." Nina turned to her daughter. "People need somewhere to live."

"But they need the dairy farms too. What's going

to happen when they all close, and this land becomes housing? It'll be just another suburban jungle like down the range."

"Emerald Hills will still be here, sweetheart," her father said. "We're not going anywhere; you're making our business too profitable for us to have any reason to sell."

Mark turned back to Justin with eyes full of understanding. "Thank you for telling us. We appreciate your honesty and openness. My offer to lease the farm is still good. I'd love to be able to buy it, but I'm sure what the developer is offering is more than we could ever afford."

The figure that Stephen had mentioned was more than most people could afford. It came with a lot of digits. Justin would be set up for life; he could stop working if he wanted to. His whole family could. The developer still had to dot some i's and cross some t's, but they had already done substantial research and planning. Stephen suggested that they had had their eye on Maleny for a long time, just waiting for a suitable property to become available.

It was hard for Justin to wrap his head around. Boyd had been dead for less than two weeks, and there was already an offer of lease on the table from Mark, and now this purchase offer.

He tried to avoid listening to the niggling whispers in the back of his mind. *What would Boyd want?*

Nina stood and opened her arms to him. He hugged her briefly and thanked her for understanding.

"I'm here if you need to talk about anything." Mark shook his hand.

Greer wished him luck before Freya walked him to the door and down the front stairs. The silence between them was almost unbearable. He wished she'd say something. Anything.

When they reached his car, he lingered at the door, wanting desperately to fix this, to touch her and tell her everything would be okay.

"Thank you for telling us." She regarded him with huge brown eyes overflowing with something he didn't want to see—disappointment.

"Everything was going so well." He reached his hand out to stroke her cheek. "We've only just begun."

She placed her warm hand over his and pressed against it, her eyes closed. "This doesn't have to be the end …"

He wanted to believe her. Maybe he would have if only she'd looked him in the eye when she said it.

He knew he should drop his hand, walk away, and leave her to get on with her life. But he was caught, held by a need he wished didn't exist. "I'm sorry. I really am."

She let go of his hand and took two swaying steps backwards. "So am I."

And with those simple words, his heart broke.

CHAPTER 12

Freya spent the night tossing and turning. Her head churned with thoughts of deceit and betrayal. But the more she thought about it, the more she came to see Justin's point of view.

As much as she didn't want another housing development taking over the precious farmland still had left in town, she could see that the responsibility of owning a farm was not something Justin wanted. And leasing it out certainly wouldn't make the same amount of money as a sale.

Freya was nothing if not determined though, so she spent the cold, early hours of the morning staring up at the ceiling, formulating a plan.

If Justin was going to sell, she was going to make

him see exactly what he would be giving up, and how it would affect the town she loved.

After the morning milking, she ran to her car, threw her things into the back, and drove as fast as she could over to Justin's farm. If he had already left, then there would be no chance for her plan to work.

She let out a loud sigh as she drove over the rise and saw his car parked in front of the house. She pulled up beside it and climbed out of her car.

Leaves and grass, still wet from the early morning fog, glistened in the sparse sunlight. A huge cobweb adorning a bush sparkled, as if made from silver thread, and a kookaburra burst into his signature laugh from a tree close by.

Finding the door open, she let herself in, calling out a hello when she didn't see him.

"Freya?" Justin appeared from the hallway door wearing only a towel haphazardly wrapped around his hips. His chest and abdomen gleamed with water, and his hair was still damp.

Heat rose through her body as she drank him in —his dark silky hair, the line of his jaw with a five o'clock shadow, and the natural curve of his sensual lips. Lips that had loved her only yesterday.

"Sorry, I shouldn't have barged in." She half turned, unsure what to do.

He moved towards her and touched her arm. "Are you okay? What are you doing here?"

She met his eyes. "I'm sorry about yesterday, I was so rude." She swallowed. "I get it now. Farming doesn't mean the same to you as it does to me, and that's okay."

His lips curled in a smile as he stepped closer. She became acutely aware of his closeness, his size, his smell, and most of all, his understanding.

"I was so scared. I thought I'd lost you." He reached out and stroked her hair.

She let her eyes close briefly at his touch. "I don't want you to go." Opening her eyes, she let herself get swallowed up in the depths of his eyes. "I'd like to show you why your farm is so important to the community, and to me. Then if you still want to sell, that's your decision."

His hand stilled, and his body tensed. "Then what? If I decide to sell, that's it for us?"

She put her hands on his bare chest. "No, it doesn't have to be. I mean, I'll respect whatever decision you make."

"I have to go back to Brisbane. I have work and an apartment." He raked a hand through his damp hair.

"Please, can you just stay for a week? That's all I ask."

He took her hands in his, meeting her eyes with a look that was so full of hope and determination, it took her breath away. "It's a good thing I own my own business. I'll need to check in with work, but I'll give you a week. At least some of that time needs to be spent working though."

Her voice brightened, and she knew she would have accommodated anything he asked. "We can find time to work. All we need are our laptops and Wi-Fi."

She ran her hands up and around his neck, revelling in the feeling. Then she kissed him. It was a soft, gentle kiss. It started slowly and built with heat and desire. She felt his hands move across her back and down her spine, until they were cupping her bottom. The towel between them dropped and his uncovered manhood pressed against her.

He pulled back and gave her a smouldering look that was so intense, she practically melted right there and then.

"Bloody hell." His voice was thick with lust. "You should come with a warning."

Freya felt a glow of pride.

After working up a sweat in the bedroom, Justin and Freya showered, dressed, and set up their laptops at the dining room table. Freya had had the foresight to pack hers before coming over. This was just another sign of how well she already knew him.

Justin watched her over the screen of his laptop. He loved looking at Freya, with her smooth, sun-kissed skin and thick blonde hair. He felt so lucky that she had chosen him to spend her time with. He didn't know what he had done to deserve it, but he was oh, so thankful.

She smiled, her eyes soft and lovely.

His heart flipped over. *Shit*. He needed to pull himself together. The sooner he finished his work, the sooner he could taste those sweet lips again.

For hours they banged away on their computers, every now and then sharing something of interest— a Facebook comment, or picture on Instagram. Finally, he leaned back in his chair and stretched his arms. The sun was shining, covering the pastures with its golden warmth.

"I think we deserve a break." Freya closed her laptop. "How about lunch and some sightseeing?"

He shot her a cheeky grin. "I'm all yours."

She pushed her chair back and came around to wrap her arms around him from behind. Her arms draped around his chest, her cheek against his. She smelt so good, felt so good, and with a single touch, she made him turn to mush.

It wasn't fair that a woman could have this much pull on a man.

He pulled her onto his lap and kissed his way across her cheek to her ear where he nibbled at her lobe, before leaving it to kiss a trail down her neck. She felt too good in his arms, her curves moulding against him as she pressed closer and moaned against his mouth. That sound was his undoing.

When they finally left the house in search of food, Justin found himself seeing the world in a whole new light. The cows were grazing contentedly and chewing their cud, enjoying the full sun after the cool night. It was peaceful and quiet. A perfect country setting.

Freya drove them out of town. Instead of heading to the main street, like he was expecting, she turned down Mountain View Road. The street was lined with a mix of old and new houses, many architecturally designed, with neatly pruned formal gardens. The houses on the left were built on downward-sloping blocks, and behind them he saw their magnificent view of the mountains and hills below.

Freya slowed and flicked the indicator before turning, taking them past a sign welcoming them to the Mary Cairncross Scenic Reserve. After parking the car, Freya took his hand, and they walked towards a very modern building which housed a café and other rooms.

"What is this place?" he asked, turning to take in the surrounding rainforest, playground, and wide open space where children kicked balls and cartwheeled on the soft grass.

"In the 1940s, three sisters gave this land to the council under the condition that the rainforest be preserved and never sold for residential or commercial purposes." She waved toward a sign directing them to a rainforest discovery centre. "This was redeveloped in the last few years. After we have a look, there's a beautiful trail we can walk."

He pulled her towards him with a gentle tug. "I thought we were getting lunch."

She pressed a kiss against his lips. "After our sightseeing. We have to work up an appetite."

"We already did." He ran his hands up and down her arms. "Twice."

"Trust me. You don't want to miss this." She took a step and waited for him to follow her.

They walked through the open doors of the Rainforest Discovery Centre, and Justin paused to take in the state-of-the-art interactive displays and exhibits, while Freya dropped coins into a donation box.

She showed him how cabinet drawers in the display opened, and peepholes revealed secrets of the bush. There was even an interactive movie which showed a rainforest setting in different weather conditions. As they sat watching a holograph of a wallaby grazing, he couldn't help but chuckle.

"What's so funny?" she asked.

"Is this your idea of a movie and a meal?"

She smiled and kissed him. "Welcome to Maleny."

Freya held onto his hand as they strolled through the bushwalk. She pointed out birds she heard and saw, including whipbirds, parrots, and the one bright yellow and black regent bowerbird.

When they returned to the café, his stomach was grumbling, and he happily sank into a chair at an outside table with a stunning view of the Glasshouse Mountains.

"Since you're playing tour guide, tell me about the mountains," he said, grandly waving his hand towards the hills that rose abruptly from the otherwise flat terrain.

Freya had an encyclopaedic knowledge of the town's history, locals, and nature. She smiled at him and cleared her throat. "The highest hill is Mount Beerwah, but that funny-looking one"—she pointed in the direction of a rocky hill with a long, vertical spire-shaped peak—"that's Mount Tibrogargan. They're not actually hills, but remnants of volcanic activity that happened millions of years ago."

Her voice, combined with the view of these ancient rock mountains, lulled him into a strange, mystified state.

"Captain James Cook named them 'Glasshouse Mountains' in the 1700s because they reminded him of the glass furnaces in Yorkshire."

He forced his attention back to Freya, whose gaze seemed hazy, as though she too was caught up in their enchantment. She looked so lovely like that, so at one with her surroundings and the magical qualities they had. Or maybe it was Freya who was magical and projected it onto her surroundings. He was about to comment on it when a waiter came over to take their order.

Flustered, Justin grabbed the menu and quickly scoured it. There were plenty of gluten-free, paleo, vegan, and free-range options, but he settled on the good old cheeseburger with chips and an aioli dipping sauce.

"Are you sure you don't want to swap the aioli for tomato sauce?" Freya grinned at him, before ordering herself a caesar salad.

"No, I'll take a chance on the aioli." He reached for her hands and held them in his. She rubbed her thumb across his sensitive palm, and he felt his body relax.

"Tell me about your life in Brisbane. What's it like?"

He thought of his daily routine in the bustling city, crowds of people everywhere, the pollution and garbage. "It's a whole different world from this."

"I could never live somewhere I couldn't see the stars at night."

"But don't you want to go shopping, or to a nightclub sometimes?"

She grinned. "Of course, and I do. It's only a ninety-minute drive away; we're not in the middle of the outback, after all."

"It kind of feels like it."

"It's great, isn't it? We're tucked away up here in our own little oasis. Sure, we have a thriving tourism industry, which"—she put her hand on her heart —"pays my bills, and I love it to pieces. But when the tourists go home and the weather cools down, it's just us locals left. We are the people who look after the land and nurture it for the next generation."

"Would you ever live anywhere else?"

She shrugged. "Maybe, but this will always be my home. My heart is here; so is my family. I want to raise my children here, on a farm with animals and wide open spaces." She looked at him wistfully, and he wished he had a fraction of her certainty about life.

"What do you want?" she asked in a lowered voice, so quiet he almost didn't hear her.

He squeezed her hand. He was only sure of one thing right now. "You."

CHAPTER 13

*A*fter a delicious meal, the pair drove back into town and parked on the main street. Freya took Justin's hand and enjoyed the shiver of sensation that ran up her spine at his touch. She knew the main street of Maleny like the back of her hand. The store owners were friends, and she could always count on them for a quick chat or to lend a helping hand.

They crossed the road to Tesch Park, where the children's playground was the centre of attention. Pre-schoolers played happily while their mums watched on, sipping coffee. But it was the library, still the heart of the community, that she wanted to show him, so they walked past the children and entered the old building.

"The library? Really?"

"Don't you like books?"

"I adore books, but I don't have a membership."

"Libraries are about more than just books." She gestured to the wall where large photographs of Maleny's history were on display. He stepped forward and studied them and she watched him, hoping he would feel the connection to the land, and to the history, like she did—like his father had.

"The butter factory? Butter used to be made here?"

"Yep, the building is still here. It's a vet surgery now." She led him past the stacks of books, and past the people sitting quietly reading at the tables, towards the back of the room where huge windows overlooked the river. Beautiful old trees lined the far side, and bushes helped to frame their view.

"This is the Obi Obi River. The pioneers had to build bridges to get over it. It's not very high now, because we haven't had a lot of rain, but when it does pour the river can be very dangerous."

He nodded at her and seemed to be taking in everything she said.

She led him outside and around the building, where a low pathway wound under the main road, right along the riverbank.

"There are platypuses in the river. If you come

here at dusk, or very early morning, you can see them."

He paused to look out on the narrow river. It was flowing steadily over rocks and through reeds. "I've never seen a platypus before."

"They're so cute. They dive and splash around— it's fun to watch."

"Where are we going now?" he asked as they walked back up to street.

"To the supermarket. I noticed you need a few things."

A short stroll later, they walked in through the open, welcoming doors of the independent supermarket. As usual, it was a hive of activity, the checkouts busy and lots of people pushing trolleys up and down aisles.

"I don't think I need milk," he said when she paused in front of the fridge.

"I know. I just wanted to show you what they stock." She pointed to the display of milk in various-sized containers with the familiar Emerald Hills logo displayed on them. "Milk from your cows goes into every bottle that we sell. It goes into the cream, the yogurt, and the cheese." She paused. "You can find Emerald Hills products everywhere as far as Toowoomba, the Gold Coast and Rockhampton.

People all over south-east Queensland consume milk made right here in Maleny. From Boyd's animals. You should be proud of that; I sure am." She turned slightly to show him where the yogurts and cheeses were kept. "The strawberry yogurt is my favourite."

She handed him a single-serve tub, which he accepted and stared at the Emerald Hills logo of jagged hills and a cartoon cow.

"My mother designed the logo. It was supposed to be a joke, but we decided it captured the essence of what our business is all about. From our family to yours—that's our core value."

"It's really good. I didn't know your mum was an artist."

Freya thought of the times she had caught her mother drawing on serviettes and edges of the newspaper. "She likes to dabble, but she doesn't get a lot of time to pursue it."

They walked slowly through the aisles, and Freya pointed out other local produce, including strawberries, pineapples, macadamia nuts, and a wide variety of meat. Justin stopped to read labels and put various things in his trolley.

As they loaded their products on to the checkout conveyor, Freya chatted to Margie, their cashier. It wouldn't take long for news of their outing to become widespread knowledge around town. People had already seen them together plenty the last few days, not to mention at the pub. Tongues would be wagging, but she didn't care. The more time she spent with Justin, the more her feelings for him grew.

Of course, that would make it harder when it came time for him to leave. Would they be able to make a long-distance relationship work? Would he even want to try?

She pushed the thoughts away. She needed to focus on the present, not the what-ifs. They were together now, and that was all that mattered.

He was facing a big decision, and she knew it would be a hard one to make. She could only hope that during this week, he would fall in love with the farm, the community, and maybe just a little bit with her.

CHAPTER 14

*J*ustin and Freya had finished unpacking the groceries, and putting things away in the kitchen, when there was a knock on the door.

Justin turned to see Fred waiting for him. "Afternoon."

"Sorry to bother you." Fred looked from Justin to Freya but didn't make a comment. "We've got an orphaned calf down in the shed."

Freya moved beside him. "Is it a newborn?"

Fred nodded. "A big one too. Looks like there was some problems birthing and the mother didn't make it."

"Is the calf okay?" Justin asked.

"Should be fine. She's in a nice, dry pen."

Freya touched his shoulder. "You must be tired. We'll look after her tonight; you head home."

Fred gave her a weary smile, and Justin realised he must have been on the job for more than twelve hours. "That's right. We'll look after the calf."

"I appreciate it. She'll need a feed in a little bit."

"Don't you worry about anything. Go home and get a good night's sleep." Freya waved him home before turning back to Justin. "Looks like you've got yourself a poddy calf."

"A what?"

"An orphaned calf is called a 'poddy calf'. Now let's go and find a bottle and give her a feed."

They put on their boots and walked down to the milking shed, where Freya hunted around for a bottle and teat.

After finding them, she filled the bottle up from a tanker and secured the teat on top. The calf was alone in a pen, bleating hungrily when they found her.

Freya murmured softly and offered the calf the bottle. It was apprehensive at first then, with a little coaxing, took the teat in its mouth and sucked hungrily.

"Your turn." She offered Justin the upturned bottle.

Justin shook his head and stepped back. "I've never done it before."

"There's nothing to it. Just take the bottle and hold it at this level.

He took the bottle from her and held on as the calf pushed and pulled on the teat until the bottle was empty.

"Does she need more? How do you know that's enough?"

"She's a newborn so we just fed her colostrum and that's all she needs today. Soon she'll go on the milk feeder with the other calves."

Justin took in the size of the black and white calf. "*She's* a newborn? She's huge."

"Usually they're born at around 30 kilograms. This one's a lot bigger though. I'm not surprised the mother didn't make it," Freya said as she cleaned the bottle, and left it to dry on the sink.

He shouldn't have been surprised. This was a working farm—animals were born and died every day. It was part of the life cycle. Fundamentally he knew this, but being here, seeing it in person, made it really sink in.

He watched Freya as she dried her hands on a towel. Her hair was swept up in a top knot and she looked sexy as hell, even in her muddy black gumboots.

It wasn't just the farm.

She made him more aware of life, of love than he ever had been before.

Justin was bone-cold and shivering as he finished spraying the antiseptic on the last of the cups and put the spray away for the following morning.

Freya had slept over last night and woken him early, insisting they help with the morning milking, despite the cold rain that had pelted down consistently overnight.

The sound of rain hitting the iron roof drowned out all sounds as the last of the animals left the stalls with full bellies and empty udders.

"You look like you could use a warm shower," Freya said, a healthy blush on her cheeks, and a satisfied grin on her face.

He nodded. "A shower would be great."

They let Fred know they were going, before turning up the collars on their jackets and facing the wet, grey day.

"Want to make a run for it?" Freya asked.

"Do you think it will ease?" He looked towards the clouds, dark and thick.

"The alternative is to stay down here."

He glanced around. "I don't think I can get any colder than I already am."

She took his hand in hers, and they started running. Freya's boot got caught halfway to the house and she slipped forward, causing Justin to lose his balance as well, until they both fell flat on their backs in the mud. The cold rain sluiced down their faces. He rolled over and looked at Freya. She was laughing, despite the rain soaking her.

He chuckled, and stood and wiped his muddy hands on his jeans, before offering one to her. She grabbed his hand and let him help her up, still laughing as the rain soaked her hair and clothes further.

"What's so funny?" He wiped mud from her cheek.

"This is," she replied. "You and me out here while it's raining. Don't you love the rain?" She leaned back and opened her mouth.

He couldn't help but watch in awe, admiring her free spirit and nature-loving attitude. So instead of being smart, and running up to the house, he pulled her closer to him and kissed the smile right off her face. The passion built between them. Freya turned serious and took his hands in hers. Together, they sprinted the final distance back to the house.

They discarded their dirty boots and jackets at

the door. He leaned in and claimed her mouth with a searing kiss. It was slow, and hot, and deep; his body pressed her back against the wall, so she could feel every solid, taut, inch of him.

He felt like a man possessed, and nothing in the world could have kept him from her. He carried her to the bathroom and flicked the heater on. He ran one hand down her curves and felt her tremble at his touch, and lord, he loved how responsive she was, how he could see the effect he had on her, her desire just as wild as the fire burning in his own veins. She felt so good in his arms, her curves moulding against him eagerly as she pressed ever closer.

While the water heated up, he lovingly undressed her, memorising every inch of her skin. Then she helped him out of his own clothes before they stepped into the shower together.

He soaped his hands and glided them up and down her arms and legs, across her back and belly, and over her breasts. Then he sank to his knees and tasted her core. She writhed in pleasure, pushing herself into his mouth and hands, as he worked his own kind of magic.

She pulled him up and wrapped her legs around him as he pushed himself into her. He watched her face—her eyes closed, and she appeared to be savouring every single sensation.

God, she was beautiful. And his, all his.

He cupped her chin with one hand and leaned in close. His kiss was hot and fierce, his body hard and tense, as if he could show her without words how he felt about her.

She cried out his name as they came together, a hot mess of limbs and satisfaction.

They had dried off after their shower and retreated to the warmth of the bed. Contented and happy, Justin lay on his back with Freya's body cradled against his side, her head on his chest.

"I wish we could stay here all day." Her voice was wistful.

"Me too." He drew lazy circles on her back with his fingertips.

She rested her chin on him, and she looked at his face. "I have to get up though. I have to prepare for the ag show this weekend."

He frowned. "What ag show?"

"The Maleny Agricultural Show is on this Friday and Saturday."

"Is that like the Brisbane Ekka, with rides and show bags?"

She giggled. "Yes, but on a much smaller scale.

This is just a country show with more of an emphasis on the animals and machinery than sideshow alley and fairy floss."

He smiled at her as he said teasingly, "But just so I've got this correct, there will be dagwood dogs, right?"

"Yes, there will be dagwood dogs." She climbed on top of him, straddling his hips. "I can't believe you like them. They're just a sausage on a stick, covered in batter and fried."

In between kisses, he murmured back at her, "Not all of us were raised with chefs in the family."

She started nibbling his neck, kissing down his chest.

"What else can I expect from this show?"

"Dad is one of the cattle judges"—she licked, and nibbled, and sucked—"and Greer is entering the cake-decorating competition."

He groaned as she teased one of his nipples. "Are you entering anything?"

"No, but I'm running a stall for Emerald Hills. We'll have samples and kids' activities."

"Will you be busy the whole time?" His mind was starting to cloud over with desire, and he didn't know how much more he could take.

"I'm sure I'll be able to get away for a little while and show you some of the show highlights." Her hand headed south, and he gasped as she clenched him.

"There's a rodeo on Saturday night and fireworks," she said casually. "It'll be fun."

Justin was breathing deeply, practically gasping, as she moved her hand up and down. "I know something else that's fun."

"Umm ..." She exhaled as she wriggled her way down his body and took him between her teeth.

He sank back onto the bed and thanked his lucky stars he had stayed in town.

CHAPTER 15

*J*ustin sipped his coffee and looked out the window. The rain had been falling consistently all night and puddles had formed on the dirt driveway.

Freya had finally forced herself to leave Boyd's place with the promise of meeting up later in the day. He admired her dedication to her work and her family. He was finding it hard to find things about Freya Montgomery that he didn't like.

Without her there, the silence in the house was deafening. Already he missed her smile, her laugh, and her touch. What was it going to be like when he left?

The prudent thing would be to leave before he became any more involved with Freya and her family. But the thought of doing so wrenched his heart so painfully, he couldn't stand it.

He turned back to his laptop. Working here was impossible without her, so he saved his document and closed the lid. Maybe a change of scenery would help. He grabbed his car keys and opened the front door. He shivered when icy wind smacked into his face, chafing his lips and making the tip of his nose ache. He climbed into his car, dialled up the heater, and rubbed his hands together.

He drove carefully along the muddy driveway, trying not to get bogged. He understood now why all the locals owned four-wheel-drives.

Turning onto the main road, he decided to explore more of the town and see where people lived. He was also curious to see the golf club, which he had heard talk of at the pub.

He surveyed the landscape. It seemed suburbia had crept its way farther out of town than he had expected. He turned down a narrow, built-up street. The sleek bitumen road extended into the distance. Driveways intersected it every few metres, leading to identical-looking houses which were built so close together they were practically touching.

He recalled what Stephen had said—that there was a lot more money in subdivision than running a few cows. People liked their big houses and small bits of dirt, and there was a shortage of affordable housing in Maleny and the rest of the Hinterland.

He was accustomed to this sort of overcrowding in the city, used to apartment buildings and gated communities. But after living in Boyd's house, surrounded by acreage, the housing estate made him feel claustrophobic.

He found his way back to the main street and soon enough saw signs to the golf club. It was empty today—the rain must have been keeping people indoors. His stepfather was a golf-lover, and Justin had played the occasional game with him. The Maleny Golf Course was small and hilly, but he knew Geoff would have enjoyed the challenge it presented.

He continued driving and noticed a sign in front of an old house declaring it Pattemoor House, an historic property. It was a colonial-designed, single-storey house with a wide wrap-around veranda. He remembered seeing an early photograph of it in the library when Freya took him there. He smiled to himself, and silently congratulated the historical society for preserving it and keeping it in such good condition.

Back in town, he pulled up in front of a café

advertising his new favourite—Maleny Coffee. He grabbed his laptop and headed inside.

The café was one of many on Maple Street, but its hanging plants and bohemian furnishings drew him in. The tables were all filled with couples and groups chatting over coffee, and huge platefuls of delicious-looking food.

At the counter, he was served by a woman wearing a black apron and a friendly smile. She glanced at his laptop. "We have a loft upstairs. It's quieter there if you need to get some work done."

"Perfect," he said and ordered the big breakfast and a large flat white.

He poured himself a glass of water from a jug on the counter before starting up the stairs. He was pleasantly surprised to find a spacious, light room with only a few people occupying tables. The walls were covered in framed pictures of plants and shelves full of greenery and books. He chose a table by a window and set up his laptop.

The hum of the coffee machine and people chattering downstairs did nothing to distract him from the work he had been procrastinating from. He took a break from the app he was designing when his big breakfast arrived. It was piled full of crispy bacon, sausages, potato rösti, mushrooms, a fried egg, and tomato.

"Are you Justin?" The same lady who had taken his order and delivered his meal asked.

He looked at her with raised eyebrows. "I am."

"Don't look so surprised. You know you can't hide in a small town," she said with a smile. "I'm Meredith. I went to school with Freya."

He shook her hand. "Nice to meet you. Is this your place?"

"It is." She put her hands on her hips and looked around proudly.

"It's got a great vibe about it, and the food looks amazing."

"I hope you enjoy. It's hard competing with Greer, but we all do pretty well. Let me know if you need anything and enjoy your meal."

"Thanks." He smiled at her before she headed back down the stairs.

He couldn't help himself groaning as he took his first bite. He savoured every morsel and surprised himself at how quickly he got through it.

"He's upstairs," Meredith said with a wink as she accepted the cartons of milk Freya had brought her. She didn't usually do the deliveries, but when Meredith had casually mentioned Justin was at her café, Freya had insisted she bring the milk right over.

Freya pretended to look shocked. "Who is?"

"You know very well who." Meredith glanced around before leaning in conspiratorially. "He's a looker, too. If you hadn't already called dibs, I might have made a play for him myself."

"Meredith! What would your husband say?" Freya scolded her with a smile. Meredith had married straight out of high school and had never admitted to regretting it.

"I'm allowed to look. He's sweet, too. He's been here for hours drinking coffee and he enjoyed my big breakfast. So, tell Greer she's got to up her game."

Freya blew her friend a kiss and climbed the stairs to the loft. She paused at the top to watch Justin. He was angled sideways to her with his head down, staring at the computer screen, his fingers tapping lightly on the keyboard. He was so focused on what he was doing.

As though he sensed her watching, he paused and turned in his seat to find her staring.

"Hey, you," he said as she walked towards him.

"Hi." She kissed him on the cheek before slipping into the chair opposite. "Meredith tells me you've been here all morning. Have you got lots of work done?"

He nodded. "I have, and don't tell Greer, but the food here is really good. Even the gluten-free things."

"Are you ready for a break? It's stopped raining; we could take a walk."

"Sounds good. I need to burn off some of those calories." He packed up his laptop and followed her down the stairs. They stopped at the counter to pay, and Meredith insisted he come back anytime he needed some peace and quiet. Then, when Justin's back was to her, Meredith caught Freya's attention and gave her two enthusiastic thumbs up.

They walked down the street together, stopping to gaze at window displays, and chat about the things for sale. The lolly shop had an interesting display of exotic and international sweets. The second-hand bookstore had Australian historical novels in the window and across the road there was an art gallery which they explored. They took their time, pointing out and discussing their favourite pieces. Freya had always loved the clay artwork made by another local friend of hers.

But it was in the bookstore, set in a beautiful art-deco style building, that they spent most of their time perusing—everything from the new releases, to the self-help and gardening sections, to the children's section with its bright colours and comfy furniture.

"Has this bookstore been here for a long time?" he asked her.

"As long as I can remember. It's changed owners a few times though."

"I think I remember it from my childhood."

Her heart leapt. She desperately wanted him to feel a connection to the town, and a childhood memory could do that for him. "I remember Mum saying that we would come here for playgroup, especially in winter. Maybe your mum brought you here?"

"She didn't make many friends; that was part of the reason why she left. She didn't have any support."

"That must have been hard for her. Alone with a baby, a husband who was always working, and no close friends." Freya said thoughtfully.

He gave the smallest of shrugs.

"I've spent many, many afternoons in here. It's my favourite shop in town." She caressed a shelf full of novels.

"I can see why."

They left the warmth of the bookstore and continued walking until they had seen both sides of Maple Street.

"I should let you get back to work," she said, even though she didn't want to leave him. She enjoyed their time together so much, even when they were just walking around talking.

"If I'm going to take Friday off to help you at the ag show, then I really do need to get more done today." He sighed. "Come over tonight?"

His hand rested on the curve of her back and his touch was so soft, so intimate, and so suggestive.

The hairs bristled on the back of her neck as she leaned into him and whispered in his ear, "What did you have in mind?"

"We could stay in and get food delivered."

"Sorry, no one delivers up here. But I can pick something up, or better yet, we can cook something together."

"I like to eat food but I'm not a great cook," he confessed.

"When you live with Greer and Nina Montgomery, you pick up a few things." She smiled. "We'll do something simple."

"Simple and fast," he said and kissed her cheek. "There are other things I'd rather spend time doing with you tonight."

She kissed him and ran her hands over his shoulders. "There are plenty of fun things we can do in the kitchen."

"In that case, maybe you should bring some cream with you."

She kissed him again and reluctantly let him go. She felt like skipping all the way back to her car. It had been hard enough to get any work done this morning and now, with those kinds of thoughts in her mind, she wondered how she would accomplish anything for the rest of the day.

CHAPTER 16

*F*reya knew from past years that people always arrived early, eager to order their breakfast rolls and buy their show bags before they sold out.

The Emerald Hills exhibit was on the main field, which the soccer club usually played on. They had erected a giant, white marquee to cover their displays of cheese, milk, and yogurt as well as photos and an informational movie playing on repeat. This year, they also had a fenced-in children's area with ride-on sheep and cow toys. Bales of hay were strategically placed so parents could get a coffee from the Maleny Coffee vendor next door, then sit and rest while their children played.

With a pause in the festivities, Freya walked outside the marquee to survey the rest of the exhibits. Strong smells of animals and fried food wafted through the crowds of lively people, all enjoying a sunshiny day. It was very different to the previous year when it had rained so hard the grounds had taken weeks to recover, and the soccer teams had had to postpone their home games.

She waved and greeted neighbours and friends as they passed and smiled, and she watched eager children begging their parents for rides, prizes, and fairy floss.

But it all faded as she saw Justin strolling toward her. His gait was relaxed and loose, so different to when she had first met him. He had been as jumpy as a kangaroo then. Now, it was as though a cloud had lifted and his true self was shining through.

She jumped him when he was close enough, wrapping her arms around his shoulders and breathing him in. She couldn't get enough of him. He held her tightly as though it hadn't been just twenty-four hours since they had last seen each other.

"I didn't know there were this many people living in Maleny." He released her and looked at the building crowds of people.

"This is quiet. Just wait until the lunchtime rush." She took his hand and walked him back inside the marquee. He looked around, studying all the little details she had added to the space to make it welcoming and fun for people. Like the beanbags and display of farm-themed children's books, or the games of skittles people could play using Emerald Hills-branded milk bottles.

"You've outdone yourself."

His compliment made her feel warm and giddy.

"Thanks." She took him to the display of old photographs she had put up, and pointed to a black and white one in the centre. "Recognise this house?"

He studied the picture of a house with cattle in front of it and a man hard at work, building a fence. "It's Boyd's farm."

She nodded. "Anthony Wheeler built it in 1912 for his family. That's your great-grandfather."

Justin's eyebrows rose, and he leaned in to study it further.

A family chose that moment to enter the tent, so Freya went to greet them and offer them free samples while Justin pondered his family heritage.

Greer arrived at midday to relieve them. It had been a busy morning, and Freya was grateful for Justin's help. He had handed out samples and played with kids without any complaints at all. Many of her friends had commented on how much they liked him, and how happy she seemed.

They walked hand in hand down the path, stopping to browse vendors and displays. Show noise filtered across the grounds—the varying calls of livestock, screams from the stomach-tumbling rides, and squeals and babbles of hyper-excited children.

"This is so impressive. I had no idea there were so many local businesses." Justin said.

Freya smiled. "Apart from rural ventures, we have makers of skincare, make-up, art, clothing, perfumes and oils, and plenty of musicians and authors. It's a very creative town; it's not just tourism that keeps us going."

"What do you want to eat? The potato slinkies are amazing." She pointed to a food van with pictures of sliced potato curled around a long skewer. "They fry it and season it with chicken salt. It's so good." Her mouth watered at the memory.

"Let's start there. Then we find dagwood dogs."

They munched their way through potato slinkies, dagwood dogs, and a punnet of chips before heading into the pavilion.

Entering the main building, they walked slowly past entries submitted for the arts and crafts competitions. Freya smiled as she looked at the children's pictures which were mostly of farm animals, machinery and landscapes.

The adult section followed and displayed photographs, paintings, sculptures, wood-work, quilts, and other artistic wares.

"Now for the food," Freya said, throwing Justin a cheeky glance. "This is always fun."

There were several plates of jam drops and chocolate chip biscuits on display, as well as cakes and slices. Brightly coloured ribbons and certificates showed which delicacies had been awarded best in show.

"There's a men's section?" Justin pointed to the category description above an array of chocolate cakes.

"Yep. Only men can enter this category, and they get to use a packet mix."

Justin bent his head, comparing the winner's cake to the others, which all looked remarkably similar. "Do the judges get to try them all?"

"No, they are just judged on looks."

"Too bad. That one looks really yummy."

Freya opened her mouth and closed it again, before she could say something about him entering next year.

"Here we are." She paused in front of a large glass stand. Inside it stood an intricately decorated, three-level wedding cake. A first-place ribbon sat proudly beside it.

"Greer Montgomery." Justin read the label. "She won."

Freya marvelled at her sister's latest creation. "Isn't it amazing?"

"It sure is. Kind of makes me wonder what she's doing in Maleny and not taking the world by storm."

"She did that already. She's done stints in major restaurants in Melbourne, London and Hong Kong but she came back here because she loves it and she wanted a quieter life."

"And she's happy now?"

Freya glanced around to make sure no one overheard her next comments. The pavilion was quiet though and there was no one to overhear her. "She turns thirty next year, and she is pretty keen to settle down and have a baby. She would make an amazing mother, but she just hasn't met the right guy. I mean, there aren't many single men left in Maleny. Most of them get coupled up in high school."

"And she didn't meet anyone along the way?"

"She dated plenty, but never found the right guy."

Justin turned and caught her gaze, their eyes saying the things neither could speak aloud. That maybe they had been the lucky ones and had found their soulmate in each other.

They left and walked around to the poultry and animal displays. They were leaning on a fence, studying the cattle, when her father came over. "Hello, you two. Enjoying yourselves?"

"Sure am," Justin said as he shook Mark's hand. "Freya is showing me all that Maleny has to offer."

"Excellent. It's a great turnout this year," he said before turning to Freya. "How's our stall doing? Busy as usual?"

"Sure is. I'm glad we made more samples. Hopefully we'll have enough to last."

"Have you seen it?" Justin asked. "It looks amazing. It really draws people in."

Freya's cheeks warmed at his words.

"She's been taking lots of photos and videos too, which will look great on social media."

Mark smiled broadly. "I'm sure they will. Freya has an eye for detail. I'll stop by soon, but right now I have to go and do some judging."

"Good luck," Freya called as her father walked away. She turned back to Justin and smiled. "Now, how about sideshow alley?"

Justin and Freya followed the sound of thrill-seekers and squealing children to the carnival rides and games. When she stopped in front of the Ferris wheel, he froze.

"What's wrong?" Her eyes were full of concern.

He raised his gaze, taking in the height of the wheel and the flimsy carriages that swayed from it.

"Are you afraid of heights?"

He swallowed. Hard. "Just a little bit."

She wrapped her arms around him. "I'll be right here beside you, I promise. It's really not that high, and we'll get a great view of town."

He looked back at her and felt the fear dissolve.

She cupped her hands around his face and kissed him before turning and climbing into the waiting carriage. He followed her and sat beside her as the gate was closed behind them.

She placed a reassuring hand on his leg as they started the gentle circle up into the sky. He let his gaze wander out across the field and over the crowds milling around below them. Instead of fear, wonder filled him. The community, the people below, were his father's friends and neighbours. Freya's friends and neighbours. Perhaps they could be his too.

He shuffled back in his seat so he could fully see Freya beside him. Happiness radiated from her like she didn't have a care in the world.

He curled his fingers around the line of her chin.

Her mouth parted, her eyes widening, then he registered nothing more except the exquisite heart-walloping sensation of her soft mouth on his.

The kiss was intense, brief and laden with meaning. Exactly the way he wanted.

They made out like teenagers as the Ferris wheel circled slowly several times. It was undeniable; there was something real between them, and even if Justin didn't have all the answers yet, he couldn't hide from the truth.

Her body was soft and pliant against his, and he drew a shuddering breath as he lifted his head. He wanted to promise her he would never hurt her, that he would always be there for her, but he couldn't. Not when things were still so unsure. Not when she could change her mind about him if he accepted the sale.

If he had to, he knew that walking away from her would be the hardest thing he would ever do.

ustin spent the next day working on his laptop at Meredith's café. It was quieter than usual, with most of her clientele spending the day at the show. She paused to ask how he'd found the show, and he told her emphatically how much he'd enjoyed himself.

Then, as the night fell and the air grew crisp, he drove to the showgrounds and found Freya waiting for him at the gate, her hands full with blankets. She kissed him and led the way through the crowds that gathered on the hills surrounding the grassy arena, until they finally spotted Greer and set up their blankets next to her so they could all watch the rodeo and fireworks.

"Is it just me, or is it colder than usual?" Justin

turned up the collar of his sweatshirt, wishing he had brought another jacket.

Greer smiled at him. "Show weekend always marks the start of the cold season." She threw him a blanket, which he pulled around his shoulders, offering an arm to Freya who readily snuggled in against him.

"Aww, look at you two." Greer pulled a face at her sister.

The riders rode into the arena and were introduced. One by one, they participated in events such as calf-roping, barrel-racing and camp-drafting.

Greer, Justin, and Freya took turns buying food and drinks, and chatted to friends who wandered over. After the rodeo, they lay back on their blankets as the fireworks shot into the dark, wintry night, while country music blared from the speakers, barely audible over the cracks of the display.

Freya nuzzled in closer to Justin, who tightened his arm around her.

"Pretty cool, huh?" she asked as it finished.

"This town just keeps on impressing me."

"We aim to please." She raised her head for a kiss, which he happily gave her. "Thank you for an amazing week," she said as he cradled her in his arms.

"No, thank you. I wouldn't have known any of this existed if it wasn't for you."

Hope, trepidation, and plain desire pounded through him, and as he kissed her again he wished the night could last forever.

After breakfast the next morning, Freya set up her laptop opposite Justin's, and they both attempted to get some work done. He opened his emails and frowned when he saw one from his lawyer that he had missed on Friday afternoon. He clicked on it and read the lawyer's note advising an official offer had been made on the property.

He glanced at Freya who was concentrating hard while uploading videos from the weekend.

As the documents downloaded, he read over the terms and conditions before coming upon the amount offered.

Holy shit.

It was a lot of money. More than he had expected, even in his wildest imagination. It was enough to pay off his student loan, his sister's student loan, his parents' house, and still buy himself a new one. Hell, he could buy himself a house in Sydney with that amount of money.

This was a complete game-changer. This was life-altering.

He finished reading through the contract, searching for a reason not to accept it, anything that made it too good to be true, but he couldn't find anything that raised any red flags.

All he could think about were the dollar signs, and that these developers obviously really wanted the property.

He re-read Stephen's email, which asked him to call him at any time over the weekend for any reason. He picked up his phone and told Freya he had to make a business call. Then he went out the front door—he didn't want Freya to overhear this conversation.

The lawyer picked up on the second ring.

"I only just saw your email, or I would have called you earlier."

"No worries. What did you think? All pretty straightforward?" Stephen sounded calm and relaxed, while Justin's heart was hammering in his chest. It was like he had just won the lotto.

"Yes, I just can't believe the amount. That's a lot of money."

Stephen chuckled. "I think they will go even higher."

"Higher, seriously? I'm having trouble wrapping

my head around that figure."

"They are really serious," the lawyer said. "And they want an answer by the end of this week."

"They've done all the due diligence already?"

"Yup, they are dead-set serious and ready to settle as soon as possible."

"Okay," Justin sighed into the phone, his mind still spinning with possibilities. "I'm going to need to take a few days to think about this."

"Of course. Let me know when you're ready."

He hung up the call and put his phone in his back pocket. Then he stared out onto the fields of his father's property.

He couldn't deny that the landscape all around the Hinterland was incredibly beautiful, and the people were the friendliest he had ever met. But with that amount of money he could travel the world. He could see and do things that most people never had the opportunity to do.

But what would the developers do with this land? They would build those tiny little houses on those tiny little blocks. Concrete slabs would cover the fertile grounds that had been in his father's family for generations. They would cut and dig into earth that had never had more than grass grow on it. They would pull down the dairy and the house and all the sheds and buildings and replace them with roads and sewers and power lines.

Eventually this might be the way it had to be. But did he want to be the one to give in to commercialism?

He squeezed his eyes shut and put his hands behind his head.

It was too much. Too much depended on this one decision.

Freya.

She had said she would stand by him, whatever he decided, but would she really? What would she think of him if he sold out? Would she still be willing to be with him?

Freya smiled as she finished editing the last video from the show. It had been an amazing, busy time, and she had loved every minute of it. Being able to share the event with Justin had made it even more memorable.

He came back into the house from making his phone call, and she could sense a shift in his mood. "Everything alright?"

"Yes, fine. Want a coffee?" he asked, flicking the kettle on to boil.

"Sure." She stood and went to him.

He wrapped his arms around her. His touch rippled through her, electric. She couldn't stop the heat that rolled through her body, jolting every nerve and synapse with pure desire.

With deft fingers, she unbuttoned his shirt, and he looked at her with hot desire written into every line of his face.

"Take me to bed?" she whispered.

He swept her into his arms and kissed her with a fierceness and urgency she hadn't felt before.

CHAPTER 18

*T*hat same familiar dread curled through his system as he walked up the stairs to Freya's house. He already knew what he had to do; he just had to break the news. The coward in him had wanted to text her, leave a voicemail, but he had been raised better than that, and he had to talk to Freya and hope she understood.

She met him at the door before he had time to knock. Her face was bright and happy. But when she looked at him, and took in his solemn expression, he watched her face change. Her beautiful eyes darkened, and the corners of her mouth dropped.

He wanted to go back to yesterday, before the email, before the phone call. He felt so guilty for not telling her before they'd made love. Then she'd gone back home for a change of clothes, not before asking him to join her family for another meal. He'd agreed, knowing he wouldn't stay long enough to enjoy Greer's cooking.

"What's wrong?"

He shoved his hands in his pockets. He couldn't risk touching her and falling apart. "I got the official offer from the developers."

She leaned against the doorframe and nodded. "That's why you were acting weird. You're going to take it."

"I don't know. It's so much more than I was expecting. I don't know what to do."

She crossed her arms over her chest. "You have to do what is best for you and what you feel is right. This is your decision to make."

He nodded. Every muscle in his body wanted to reach out and pull her close. "They want an offer by the end of the week. It's a once-in-a-lifetime opportunity, but I need to get away to think about it."

"I understand." She gazed at his car, and her eyes widened at the boxes piled high in the back seat. There was no room left in his car for anything else. He was taking everything of value with him- just in case he didn't come back.

He watched as she gulped and her eyes misted over. "Well, it was fun while it lasted."

He scratched the back of his head, wanting to

promise her things he wasn't sure he could deliver. "You are a very special woman, Freya Montgomery. Don't ever forget that."

She gave a half-hearted smile. "Me? I'm just a dairy farmer's daughter." Then she reached over and gently pressed a kiss to his cheek, before pulling away, and closing the door firmly behind her.

He took a moment to steady his breathing, before walking slowly down the stairs, hoping that at any second, she would run out and stop him. But as he opened his car door and slid inside, he knew she wasn't going to come.

He started the car and put it in gear, then bumped along the muddy driveway, before turning onto the road that would lead him to the city. There was no turning back now.

CHAPTER 19

"*H*e might still agree to the lease," Mark said, as the family discussed the events over lasagne that night.

"Who in their right mind would lease out the dairy farm when they could make a lot of money from selling it?" Greer said.

"He's not just anybody. He has history here—family history," Nina said. "But it is his decision to make, and we have to trust him to make the right one."

"And if he does sell it, then we will have to make the best of the situation," said Mark, ever the optimist.

"That's right," Nina agreed, touching his hand lovingly.

Freya remained quiet, still mourning his loss, knowing in her heart she would never see him again.

"Now it's time to think ahead. We have to put this behind us and focus on other things." Nina said.

Greer slid her sister a sideways glance. Freya could think of nothing but the fact that the only man she had ever loved had just driven out of her life. She knew that for the next few days, as word spread, she would be approached by the townspeople with their pity and disappointment. Their well-meaning acts of kindness would only remind her that she had allowed herself to be vulnerable. How could she have been so stupid, when she knew it would probably end like this? She had been wrapped up in the moment and carried away. It had all been a dream. A wonderful, beautiful dream. Now, she had to return to reality, where she and her sister were still waiting for love to find them.

She tried not to feel the swell of sadness again, but it rose as steady as a tide in her chest. In time, it would be better, she told herself. In time, he would be just another detour on her path to real love.

Justin didn't want to be alone. One night in his cold apartment was enough. He wanted to be surrounded by people who loved him, who he could discuss his decision with, so he called his mum and asked if he could stay for a few days.

He pulled up in the driveway and knocked on the door.

Barbara opened it and, seeing him, pulled him into her arms. "What happened?"

"I fell in love." He shrugged.

Barbara leaned her head to the side. "I think you should come into the kitchen and tell me all about it."

He followed her to the rear of the house, past the open dining and living areas where his family celebrated every milestone and major holiday.

In the kitchen, with its sparkling surfaces and gleaming appliances, Barbara prepared two cups of coffee, and sat down next to him at the counter. "Who is she?"

"Freya Montgomery. Nina Montgomery's youngest daughter."

Barbara smiled. "I always liked Nina. I wish I had tried harder to fit in; I think she and I could have been great friends."

He wondered if there was more to the story. "Why didn't you stay with Dad? Really?"

She sighed. "After you were born, I suffered from depression. Postnatal depression is what we call it now, but back then I thought I was going crazy. You were never a good sleeper, and I would be up with you most of the night. Boyd was busy all day and needed his sleep, and after a while, I just couldn't cope."

Justin gulped down the emotion he felt—pain at having caused his mother's suffering. "So you left?"

"I hadn't had a good night's sleep in over four years. I was snappy and irritable. Boyd agreed I should take you to Brisbane and have a holiday. I could let my family help me, teach me how to look after you properly, and take you to a paediatrician." Her voice held such regret and sorrow. "A week turned into a month. I was finally getting help, and sleep, and I was scared that if I went back to Maleny it would all be for nothing. I felt like I was ruining Boyd's life. So I decided to stay in Brisbane. I called your father and told him. He didn't sound surprised. He said he had set up a bank account, and would pay as much as he could into it each week."

Justin sagged against the counter. "Just like that?"

"At the time, I didn't understand it. But since he passed, I've been thinking about it again, and I wonder if he thought he was causing the problems— if he thought he was the reason you couldn't sleep, and I was being so horrible. I don't think we'll ever know the truth, but Boyd was certainly sensitive."

It made sense why he hadn't sought out another relationship, or even close friendships, apart from Fred.

"I don't want to be like him, Mum," Justin said as his vision blurred with tears. "I want friends, a family, and to be with the woman I love."

She hugged him to her. "There is nothing more important in the world than love. I would trade everything I have for you and our family.

Justin squeezed his eyes shut.

"Now, tell me about Freya," his mother said. "Why are you here, and not up there with her?"

CHAPTER 20

*F*reya leaned back in her chair and watched as her latest video downloaded. She stretched her arms behind her. Sleep had been evading her most of the week. It was at night when memories of Justin came back to taunt her. She would toss and turn, trying to push him from her mind. But he was always there.

She turned her attention back to Facebook, where a video of yesterday's busload of schoolchildren was uploading. Their happy laughter and enthusiastic questions had helped to brighten her mood, at least for the morning. She had interviewed a few of the more charismatic six-year-olds, asking what part of the tour they'd liked the most, and what flavour yogurt they'd enjoyed. Then she had edited it into a movie.

Greer had watched the children with longing in her eyes. Her sister wanted nothing more than to be a mother; it was why she had moved back to Maleny. She would be an amazing parent, and her children would be so loved and well-treated. They'd be surrounded by family and friends, in this community that she invested in every day.

While the video downloaded, Freya scrolled down the screen before stopping abruptly on the photo of her and Justin. Her stomach clenched, but she refused to look away. She would have to overcome this sooner or later.

She had snapped the selfie during the factory tour. He looked so content and happy. Just like she had been—the perfect couple.

Her finger hovered over the delete button. If only she could delete him from her life as easily as she could delete him from her Facebook page.

The comments below drew her attention.

What a beautiful couple you make.

Thrilled to see you so happy.

Can't wait to meet him.

There were lots of emojis and love hearts too. She considered posting a comment, letting people know that they had broken up. She didn't want to hear or read his name mentioned ever again.

She appreciated that people wanted her to be happy.

She wanted to be happy.

She had been happy. So blissfully happy.

The computer pinged with a new notification.

Justin Wheeler is live now.

Damn. She knew she should have unfriended him. But he hadn't posted anything all week, and she hadn't been brave enough to look at his profile.

Another notification appeared on the screen letting her know that he had tagged both her and Emerald Hills in his live stream.

Curiosity got the better of her, and she clicked on the link. Facebook took a few seconds to load before it brought up the stream.

As the video caught up to the audio, all she could see was a frozen image of him. His chin was clean-shaven, and his short hair slightly damp.

He had dark circles under his eyes; he hadn't been sleeping either.

Finally, the audio caught up, and she played it from the beginning.

"Hi. For those of you who don't know me, my name is Justin Wheeler. I'm Boyd Wheeler's son, and when he passed away a couple of weeks ago, I found out that I'd inherited this dairy farm. I came to Maleny to put the

farm up for sale, but I didn't count on meeting so many new friends and joining such a vibrant community.

While I was there, I met a girl named Freya Mont-gomery. And if you know Freya, you know that she is an incredible, passionate woman. If I had grown up in Maleny, she would have been the girl next door. We would have played together and gone to school together. But we didn't get that opportunity because I grew up in Brisbane. But from the moment I met Freya, I felt like we were always destined to be together. It took a little bit longer than it could have, but I know in my heart that she is my soul mate and the only woman for me."

He paused, and Freya let the words sink in. His declaration of love made her heart pound.

"Freya, if you feel the same way, please come and find me."

She frowned and looked at the screen as he panned the camera slightly until she saw a familiar view. He was outside, sitting at the employee table where they had first had lunch together.

Right here at Emerald Hills.

She pushed her chair back, and threw open the door, running straight into Greer.

"Where are you going in such a hurry?"

"He's here. Justin's here." Freya took off down the hallway, barely registering that her sister was following, calling out for their parents to follow.

Freya made her way outside and paused as she took in the scene in front of her. A small crowd had gathered to watch. Justin's mobile was set up on a tripod and he stood in front of it.

Their eyes met. A hint of stubble flecked his jaw, tense with nerves, while his hazel eyes, surrounded by those gorgeously long lashes, were fixed intently on her.

She stepped cautiously closer. He had already hurt her twice—could she face a third time? Then again, neither hurt had been his fault. He had only ever been honest with her.

"What's going on?"

She turned at the sound of her father's voice. Greer hushed him and waved her parents to join the other curious onlookers.

Freya stepped past the camera. "Is it still recording?"

He nodded. "Is that okay? I can turn it off."

She shook her head. He was within touching distance now. "I don't care who sees."

She leaned forward to kiss him, but his soft words stopped her. "I didn't take the deal. I'm not selling the farm."

She blinked and gave a little shake of her head, as though she'd been far away and needed to bring herself back to Earth. "You're not?"

"No. Boyd wouldn't want me to sell to a developer. It's a dairy farm, and it'll stay that way as long as I have anything to say about it."

Their gazes remained locked, unable to break it. A gaze of yearning, of love, of hope.

Justin was back; that would have been enough for her. She reached up her arms and looped them behind his neck. "I missed you so much. Nothing felt right without you."

He buried his face in her neck, holding her with the same intensity as she held him. "I love you, Freya."

She pulled back, needing to see him when he said the words, needing to make sure she didn't imagine them. "What did you say?"

A smile spread across his face. "I said, I love you, Freya Montgomery." His voice was loud enough for everyone to hear his declaration.

She grinned. "I love you too, Justin Wheeler."

He brought his mouth to hers, and kissed her.

God, she had missed his kisses. How had she ever thought she could live without them? Without him?

Doubt and fear bubbled up in her throat. "How we going to make this work? You live in Brisbane."

"I can work from anywhere. You mean more to me than anything else. Besides who wants to live in the city when they can live here, in the heart of the Hinterland?"

She kissed him again, her heart overfilling with joy.

They broke their embrace and her family surrounded them, slapping Justin on the back and hugging her, all celebrating together.

"The farm is yours to lease if you still want it," Justin said to her father as they shook hands.

"I do. We'll take good care of it." Mark looked at him with pride in his eyes. "Your father would have been proud of you. I sure am."

"Thank you," Justin said, his voice was filled with emotion.

Freya squeezed his hand, hoping to remind him she was right beside him, and always would be.

"Look at you two, so in love." Greer wiped her eyes. She always was a sucker for romance.

Freya hugged her sister. "Your turn will come. I know it."

Greer pulled back and hugged Justin. "I don't suppose you know any single, straight men, do you?"

"Let me think about it." Justin grinned. "It'd have to be someone worthy of you."

Greer screwed up her nose. "My standards aren't that high."

Freya turned and spotted the phone. She had

forgotten it was still live-streaming. "We should turn that off."

Justin nodded. "Show's over now."

She walked behind the tripod and looked at the screen. Her mouth dropped when she saw the number of viewers. "Oh my gosh, Justin, we've gone viral."

He chuckled and tugged her hand until she was back in his arms. Back where she belonged.

"With you as the star? What did you expect?" He lowered his mouth and kissed her again.

His lips were strong and true against hers and seemed to promise a life together filled with love.

A promise of forever...

ABOUT THE AUTHOR

Bestselling author Sarah Williams spent her childhood chasing sheep, riding horses and picking Kiwi fruit on the family orchard in rural New Zealand. After a decade travelling, Sarah moved to Queensland to enjoy the endless summer, pristine beaches and tropical rainforests.

When she's not absorbed in her fictional writing world, Sarah is running after her family of four kids, three dogs and an ever growing number of chickens.

She is Founder and CEO of Serenade Publishing,

runs writers workshops and retreats, mentors and supports her peers to achieve their publishing dreams.

Sarah is regularly checking social media when she really should be cleaning.

To receive updates and free books, sign up for her mailing list.

www.sarahwilliamsauthor.com

facebook.com/sarahwilliamswriter
instagram.com/sarahwilliamsauthor
bookbub.com/profile/sarah-williams
goodreads.com/goodreadscomsarahwilliams

Their Perfect Blend

(#2 in the Heart of the Hinterland series)

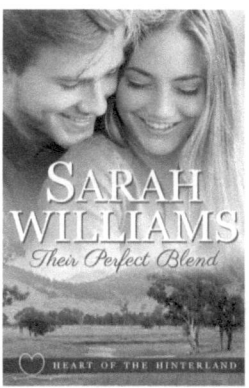

When her biological clock sets off an alarm, can she conceive a plan to give her a baby... minus the commitment?

Maleny, Australia. Greer Montgomery has enjoyed a successful career as a world-renowned chef. But after returning home just before her thirtieth birthday to run the family's farm café, she worries there's one recipe her culinary skills will never make: a child. And with few eligible bachelors her age in her tight-knit country town, she approaches her friend's handsome brother to be her baby-daddy.

Coffee roaster Hamish Pearson's dreams of a family were shattered when his girlfriend dumped him for someone else. But when he meets the gorgeous all-star chef who's just moved back, his foodie heart melts and he's instantly smitten. And though their heated romance brews quickly, he's crushed when she admits she only wants his DNA.

As Greer sorts through her conflicting feelings for the reluctant roaster, the last thing she needs is his ex meddling in their lives. And as Hamish falls harder for her, he refuses to let a contract take away his desire to be a good father.

Will Greer and Hamish whip up the perfect blend of passion and procreation for a happily-ever-after?

Their Perfect Blend is the second book in the sexy Heart of the Hinterland contemporary romance series. If you like small-town values, steamy chemistry, and complex characters, then you'll adore Sarah Williams' heartwarming story.

Buy Their Perfect Blend

The Brothers of Brigadier Station

(#1 in the Brigadier Station series)

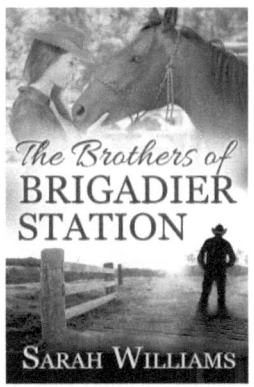

She came to the outback to marry the love of her life. She just didn't expect him to be her fiancé's younger brother.

When Meghan Flanagan, a vet-nurse from Townsville, moves to Brigadier Station in outback Queensland to marry the man of her dreams, she is shocked to discover that perhaps her fiancé isn't the man she wants waiting for her at the altar. The man she's destined to marry, just might be his younger brother.

Cautious of women after a disastrous past relationship, Darcy is happy living on his beloved cattle station, spending his spare time riding horses, going to rodeos and campdrafting. He didn't expect the perfect woman show up on his doorstep. Engaged to his brother.

With the wedding only hours away, Meghan must make the decision of a lifetime. But, her betrayal could tear the family apart. She knows all too well the pain of losing loved ones and being alone.

Now that she has the family she so desperately wants; will she risk losing it all?

Buy The Brothers of Brigadier Station

The Sky over Brigadier Station

(#2 in the Brigadier Station series)

He guards his heart. She yields to no man. Will a chance encounter set a course for true love?

Noah McGuire buries his demons deep inside. But when he's forced to return home to Brigadier Station to collect his inheritance, he can no longer avoid digging up his painful past. With the wounds of childhood trauma reopened, his world plunges into darkness until a beautiful pilot sets his heart afire.

Riley Sinclair isn't afraid to fly against the wind. While the spunky helicopter pilot's cattle herding business ruffles the feathers of most men, the handsome Noah seems different. But as demand for her skills grows, she worries that giving into passion could keep her dreams grounded.

As their chemistry soars, an unexpected tragedy throws their lives and their budding romance into a tailspin.

Can Noah and Riley leave their baggage behind to let love fly free?

The Sky over Brigadier Station is the second standalone book in the captivating Brigadier Station Western romance series. If you like flawed characters, simmering scenes, and stunning Australian and New Zealand settings, then you'll love Sarah Williams' rugged tale.

Buy The Sky over Brigadier Station

The Legacies of Brigadier Station

(#3 in the Brigadier Station series)

Can Lachie be the father Hannah needs? And the man Abbie deserves?

Lachie McGuire is trying to make a fresh start. He's sobered up and is making amends for all the people he has hurt and the pain he has caused. But some of his past actions have consequences. Even if he doesn't remember them.

Needing her independence, single-mum Abbie Forsyth accepted a nursing position in the small outback town of Julia Creek and uprooted her daughter, Hannah from the only life she had ever known. Now, in the dusty, sun burned land they are creating a life together, just the two of them.

When Lachie is injured and needs medical assistance, Abbie is there for him. She's by his side every step of the way, including letting him stay with them while he recovers from surgery. But Abbie knows how volatile life with an addict can be and she has to think about her daughter's safety above her own growing affection for the handsome grazier.

Then tragedy strikes the small rural town and secrets begin to unravel…

Return to the Outback for the third instalment in the bestselling Brigadier Station series.

Buy The Legacies of Brigadier Station

ACKNOWLEDGMENTS

My sincere thanks to all my writer friends who support and encourage me on this amazing journey. They include but are not limited to Kelly Ethan, Heather Reyburn, my awesome cover designer Lana Pecherczyk and my incredible editor Lauren Clarke and her team.

A big thank you and much love to my family for all your support and for putting up with me while I write. I love you all.

And to you, dear reader. Thank you for choosing this book to read. I know there are many other distractions and entertainment options available these days, so thank you for joining Greer, Hamish and me on this journey.

CHAPTER 1

*G*reer Montgomery shifted her mouse so the arrow on the computer screen hovered over the tab titled *Using donor sperm* and clicked.

She cruised over the myriad of headings and information before stopping on the third line. *How to choose a sperm donor.*

She clicked again, then paused. Was this really what she wanted? Letting go of the mouse, she stretched back, entwining her fingers together behind her head. She took a long, deep breath and turned away from the computer to stare out the huge windows where the first brilliant rays of sunshine poured in. Greer studied the rolling green pastures. She would never get sick of that view. It was the same view she had grown up gazing upon.

The same paddocks she had spent her childhood running through and exploring.

"Morning, sis." Freya's voice jolted Greer from her thoughts and before she could minimise the search window, her younger sister was wrapping her arms and her cow stench around her.

"Shit, Freya. Where did you come from?" She moved to close the laptop but Freya stilled her hand.

"Hey what's this?" Freya peered over Greer's shoulder and read from the website. "The reasons for people needing to access donor sperm are varied, and include heterosexual couples having difficulty conceiving because of male reproductive issues, women in same-sex relationships keen to start a family, and single women who want to have a child."

Greer sighed. "A desperate woman's last chance."

Freya and Greer had casually chatted about fertility treatments and other options Greer could consider. She was desperate to have a baby of her own, and with her thirtieth birthday only a few months away, she was hearing the clanging of her biological clock louder than ever.

"I know we joked about it the other day, but I didn't think you were really *that* serious." Freya moved to sit on the stool beside her sister.

"Look at this." Greer brought up another screen with more facts on it before reading aloud.

"According to the American Society for Reproductive Medicine, a healthy thirty-year-old woman has about a twenty per cent chance of getting pregnant each month, while a forty-year-old woman has about a five per cent chance. The reason for this is your ovarian reserve, the quality and quantity of your eggs."

"Twenty per cent? And to think that at school we were taught how to avoid getting pregnant."

Greer turned to her sister. This was serious. Her future happiness rested on what she did now. "I want at least one baby, maybe two, with a spacing of two to three years in between. I have to start now or I'm going to run out of time."

Freya reached her arm around Greer's shoulder and squeezed. "What about fate? You never know when you're going to meet *the one*. He could walk into the café tomorrow."

"Not all of us are as lucky as you." Greer hated the pang of envy she felt when she saw Freya and Justin together. Theirs had been love at first sight. Destiny and all that jazz. But Greer had never even come close to being in love. Her career had always been her first priority—cooking in a Michelin-starred restaurant, learning recipes and techniques from some of the world's best.

With that goal accomplished, she had moved on

to the next—becoming a mother. She had expected love and family to fall into place when she moved back to Maleny. But two years on, life had not played out that way at all.

"You really think someone's going to come to our farm and whisk me off my feet? I mean, there are no eligible men left in the area. Why do they all marry so young here? All the good ones are taken, and the rest have moved away."

"What about online dating then? He doesn't have to be a local."

Greer shook her head. "I love living here. We have the business and our family. This is where I want to raise my children. I don't want to have to move or have a long-distance relationship." Greer dropped her head into her hands and leaned over the kitchen bench.

She could be a single mum. It would be fine. Her family would support her, and she had enough male relatives to make sure her offspring didn't miss out on anything of testosterone importance.

"Do Mum and Dad know what you're planning?"

Greer shook her head against her hands. She wasn't ready to discuss it with her folks just yet—not until she'd made her final decision. They'd support her no matter what decision she made.

"Well, whatever you decide to do, Justin and I are here for you. We love you."

Greer raised her head and looked at her sister with her big brown eyes and kind features. Justin was a lucky man. "When's he back from Brisbane?"

"This afternoon." Freya's face brightened with that lovesick glow.

"That's nice he's home for the weekend. I am so happy for you." Greer smiled and busied herself preparing breakfast as Freya talked about their upcoming plans.

Freya had recently moved in with Justin at his house next door, but she got awfully lonely when he wasn't there, so often stayed with her family while he was away.

"We have a plumber coming tomorrow. I can't wait for the bathroom refit," Freya said. The simple house was in desperate need of renovations and the couple were excited to make it their own. The dairy farm that it sat on was being leased by Greer's family, and had proven a profitable business decision for the Emerald Hills empire.

Justin wasn't a farmer and had never pretended to be one. He had recently turned down a huge offer on his late father's property in order to keep it as a working dairy farm. It had been a startling move, but he didn't seem to regret it.

Greer loved being a part of their family business. Moving home to open the café had been a big decision, but it had been the right one for her. The hustle and bustle of the big cities had finally surpassed Greer's country-girl tolerance, and after a decade, enough was enough. Now she was home and her café was doing a brilliant trade bringing in hungry tourists after their farm tour or cheese tasting. The only thing missing was a man to share her life with and children to watch grow. She could only wish that she might one day meet someone who made her as happy as Justin made Freya.

She couldn't deny her envious thoughts that her younger sister had met her soulmate before her. And while she still dreamed of one day meeting someone, the yearning to have a baby far outweighed snatching Mr Right first.

Greer's heart sank a little more as she poured the batter for the pancakes into the heated pan. "Go wash up, will you? As much as I love your perfume of choice, it does not make for a great aperitif before breakfast."

Freya playfully poked out her tongue before heading to the bathroom.

Left alone to finish cooking, Greer's thoughts returned to her current dilemma.

Would she ever hold her own child in her arms?

Or would she end up being the single aunty who baked special treats and birthday cakes for her nieces and nephews? The spinster sister surrounded by all her cookbooks and fancy kitchen appliances but with no family of her own.

No. This was the twenty-first century. Women had babies on their own all the time and she was a strong, independent woman who could do anything she set her mind to. It was time to stop dreaming and start acting. Being a mother had always been in her plan. It was the next step in her life, and something she desperately wanted.

Even if it meant doing it on her own.

Greer reversed into the angled parking spot on Maple Street, right in front of Meredith's coffee shop. It been a busy day at Emerald Hills, with a bus full of tourists to feed and many travellers enjoying the cooler country air and farm activities offered.

People were starting to leave town now, their cars loaded with shopping bags, no doubt having visited the art galleries and antique shops. Things rarely slowed down in the small hinterland town— not even in the winter months.

The late afternoon sun warmed her back as

Greer lifted the trolley from her car and stacked two crates of milk, boxes of yoghurt, and cheese onto it—all produced at Emerald Hills. She pushed the trolley down the side alley and stopped abruptly when she came face-to-face with a large black dog who lay sprawled across the open back door.

She moved gingerly toward the dog. It looked quiet enough, but it was a big dog. A very big, shaggy dog.

"Hi there." She tried for confidence as she nudged it with her foot. "Can you move out of the way so I can wheel this stuff inside?"

The dog raised its huge black head and took its time eyeing her off, as if wondering if she was worth the effort it would take to move.

Greer chewed on the inside of her mouth, wondering if it would just be easier to go in through the front, when the dog suddenly launched itself upright. Standing, he was even bigger than she'd imagined, and she instinctively took a step backwards. He moved toward the trolley, stretching his hind legs as he went, before stopping to sniff the cartons.

"Thank you," Greer said as she reclaimed the trolley and pushed it past the animal, hurrying to get inside before it changed its mind and chased after her. When had Meredith gotten a dog? And why on earth had she chosen this one?

"Hello," she called out when she was safely inside the kitchen.

Meredith's flushed face popped around the corner. "Hey! Good timing. We just locked the front door." She cleared the path for Greer to push the trolley in front of the fridge in the pantry.

"When did you get Hagrid?" Greer motioned over her shoulder at the drooling beast. The dog was watching them, his head cocked as he let go of a soft whine.

"You lie yourself right back down, Hercules." Meredith waved a finger and the dog politely obeyed her command.

"Don't mind him. He's my brother's dog." A smile tilted the corner of Meredith's mouth. "Why don't you join us for a cuppa?"

"Us?" Greer sneaked a peek through the kitchen serving window. The chairs were stacked in neat piles by the door and Greer couldn't see anyone else.

"Yeah, Hamish brought over my coffee order. He doesn't go anywhere without Herc these days. Go through. I'll just put these away." She started unpacking the tubs of yogurt.

"Okay." Greer could use a coffee after the day she'd had. She made her way past the kitchen and into the front of the shop. She loved Meredith's bohemian décor with hanging green plants and groovy artwork. Emerald Hills was decorated with more of a traditional homestead feel with historical photos and antiques for visitors to study.

Behind the serving counter, she saw the man's profile as he busily cleaned the industrial coffee machine. The rolled-up sleeves of his flannel shirt revealed strong arms, with what looked like symbolic tattoos on his left arm.

"Hi," Greer said as she passed the empty cake display on the counter.

He turned to look at her with large caramel eyes, the same colour as the toffee sauce she poured over her sticky date puddings.

"Hi. Can I help you with something?" he asked in a deep, sexy voice which caused goose bumps to rise on her arms.

"I'm Greer Montgomery. I just dropped off some milk from Emerald Hills and Meredith invited me for a coffee." She studied his face, noting the family resemblance between the siblings and wondering why she had never met him before. Unless she had and didn't remember him? Then again, his was a face any woman would remember with his moulded cheekbones, the firm angle of his jaw, and the long, dark lashes framing those eyes.

Yep, she was pretty sure she'd remember him.

"So, you're Greer?" He smiled as he wiped his hands on his jeans before turning and extending one for her to shake. "I'm Hamish Pearson."

Greer sucked in her breath as his palm connected with hers. She watched as the colour of his cheeks deepened in the same way she was sure hers did.

"It's nice to meet you." The words tumbled from her lips.

Their hands held a fraction longer than etiquette required and he let go suddenly as the coffee machine beeped, breaking the odd trance which had begun to take hold of her.

Hamish turned his attention back to the machine. "What'll you have?"

"Flat white, thanks," Greer said as she backed away from the counter.

Meredith strolled into the room dusting crumbs from her apron.

"Busy day?" Greer asked her friend.

"Sure was. You too?" Meredith sat heavily at a table and motioned for Greer to sit next to her

"Yep, but busy is good." Greer sat across the table from Meredith before sneaking a glance at Hamish.

Meredith caught her looking. "You know my little brother, don't you? He's the man behind Maleny Roast'd."

Greer sat up straighter and raised her eyebrows. "That's you! You're responsible for my caffeine addiction. I love that stuff." Some days she felt like she lived purely on coffee, and Maleny Roast'd was her preferred brew. "We sell it at the farm too. It's very popular."

Hamish sent her a humbled smile. "Glad you enjoy it."

A memory of a boy from her childhood suddenly popped into her head. "You were a few years behind us at school, weren't you?"

He came around the counter and placed two cups of coffee on the table. "That's right. We were on the same bus."

Greer nodded slowly. "I remember you now."

Meredith pushed a cup toward her. "There you go—just the way you like it."

Greer lifted the cup to her lips and closed her eyes, allowing the rich, earthy aroma to drift up her nose at the same time as sharp, roasted freshness ran over her tongue and slid down her throat. Bliss.

She couldn't help the moan of pleasure that escaped her lips. "God, it's even better when he makes it."

Meredith giggled and Greer's cheeks burned.

Hamish joined them a moment later, a cup in his hands, and sat opposite her. He smelled a tantalising mix of coffee and hard work. She hid her face behind the cup and willed her heart to stop pounding.

"Greer is the woman who can out-cook and out-bake any pro from here to Melbourne and back … and she has the awards to prove it." Meredith bragged of her friend. Although both were chefs, neither felt the need to compete for accolades or business. There was plenty to go around.

"So, I've heard." Hamish leaned back in the chair and crossed one long leg over the other. "I've grabbed takeaway from Emerald Hills a few times when I do deliveries. I really enjoy your quiches and pies."

Greer frowned. He delivered the coffee and she hadn't seen him? Then again, she was always so focused on cooking she rarely left the kitchen.

She tried to recall what she knew of her friend's little brother. They hadn't been in the same circle of friends, and she only vaguely remembered him from childhood play dates.

Then she remembered one late, drunken night not too long ago with Freya. Her sister had pulled out pen and paper and listed all the men under forty who still lived in Maleny. Hamish's name had been on it, but Freya had also admitted sheepishly that he was with Sloan Greenwood.

Greer slid him a sideways glance. She couldn't see a ring on his left hand, but that didn't mean anything these days. He was handsome and his features were kind. A girl would be silly to let such a man go.

Greer mentally shook herself. She had made up her mind. Baby first, boyfriend later.

"I should get going." She stood, clumsily bumping the table in her haste to stand. "Sorry."

Greer didn't miss the amused expression that crossed her friend's face.

"Let's catch up again soon. We have so much to discuss," Meredith said with a wink.

She smiled back at her before turning to Hamish. "Thanks again for the coffee."

There was that smile again, just a hint of it, and she strode away quickly before it did things to her libido.

Like remind her she had one.